CONTACT

CONTACT
NEW EDEN BOOK 1

JESSICA MARTING

SHADOW PRESS

Contact (New Eden Book 1)

ISBN 978-1-989780-33-6

Edited by Autumn Reed

Cover art by German Creative

Content notes: Discussion of a natural disaster and mass casualty event; parental death.

For all my cyborg aficionados out there.

THE NIGHT SKY glowed with electricity, reminding Hannah of the stories her grandmother used to tell her about life in the old world, of its legendary storms. She halted on the crumbling stone sidewalk, a large basket of vegetables in her hands as she stared at the sky. But no rain fell, nor thunder boomed. It didn't look like any kind of lightning Hannah had ever seen. It spread its neon-bright arms in concentric circles, crackling with life as it descended toward the ground. She blinked, sure she was hallucinating from lack of sleep, then looked back at the lightning.

Nope, it was definitely still there. And it *definitely* wasn't lightning. A large saucer-shaped craft came into view, studded with hundreds of other tiny lights.

A spaceship?

Had the prayers of New Eden been answered? Had someone finally heard their distress call, launched so many weeks ago, pleading for help after being devastated by an earthquake? Despite the spaceship's welcome appearance, Hannah still had to swallow the lump in her throat that formed whenever she thought of the disaster. Two years had since passed, although it felt like decades. The quake had killed half of New Eden's population and decimated what was left of its struggling infrastructure.

Every light on the ship flared to life, a tremendous boom sounding in the air as it descended. The ground beneath her feet vibrated with the impact, reminding her of the quake. Her vegetable basket fell from her hands, scattering carrots on the dusty ground.

She forced herself to move, to run to the saviors who'd heard her call. The ship had landed in an untended field, far from the old makeshift launchpad the original colonists had constructed, but Hannah supposed it didn't matter. What time hadn't destroyed of the old launchpad, the earthquake did, and this ship looked to be too large for it, anyway. Besides, hadn't she mentioned in her SOS that any rescuers could land in the field?

As she reached the ship, its exterior door yawned open, and a ramp extended from it. She froze a few meters away, a thousand thoughts tumbling through her mind. She wasn't New Eden's mayor—he had died in the earthquake. Not knowing where she should look, she glanced down at her feet. In the light offered by the twin moons overhead and the ship's lights, she could see the poor condition of her sandals, the leather worn thin and cracking in spots. What a professional first impression she was about to make to the planet's first visitors in, well, *ever*.

Light spilled out from the ship's hatch, bright enough to make her squint. Just as quickly, it was blocked by a huge figure, who paused at the top of the ramp. She couldn't make out their features, only a body that towered over hers.

Hannah's stomach dropped, but she forced herself to

walk closer to the ship. She waved her arms to catch their attention. "Hello!"

It worked. The figure walked down the ramp, heavy boots clanging off its surface. She swallowed. They sounded like they could do a lot of damage. "Hello," she repeated. "Welcome to New Eden. I apologize for the lack of hospitality. Did you get my message?" Her mind flashed back to her weeks of secret work as she rebuilt a transmitter to broadcast her SOS. Months had passed without a response, so long that she had quietly despaired that she might have failed.

The figure strode off the ramp and across the grass, headed straight for her. Hannah didn't move, although a small voice told her it might be a smart idea.

But what if the ship's occupants were here to help? Had they heard the distress signal she'd broadcasted across her corner of the galaxy? It wouldn't be polite to run back to New Eden's ruined city if they were responding to her SOS. If they had the technology to build such a ship, they had the technology to help the planet's survivors rebuild their lives.

The figure stopped a meter away from where Hannah stood. This close, she could see it was a man, wearing a black suit that better resembled armor than clothing. He'd strapped a weapon to his hip, although Hannah didn't know enough about them to identify it. His hair and ears were covered by a helmet that hugged his scalp, leaving only his face visible. The twin moons and light offered by his ship highlighted his sharp cheekbones and dark eyes that fixed on Hannah.

She didn't know what else to do after welcoming him to New Eden, so she gave him a small wave.

He regarded her coolly for a few seconds, but he didn't draw the weapon at his hip. Maybe he didn't think she was enough of a threat to do so. "Are you the leader of this place?" His voice was rough and deep.

The words were encouraging, even if the voice was a little intimidating. "Did you get our distress signal? We sent it out over, oh God, like two months ago, maybe? I've sort of lost track of time." The words slipped out before she could better refine them. "Not that I don't appreciate your arrival. We had a natural disaster and lost many of our people. Thank you for coming, all the same. I'm not sure where you want to help us start rebuilding, but we have a power grid that's in desperate need of repair. Maybe we . . ."

He cut her off. "Are you Hannah Forsyth? Your voice is registering as the same one that sent a message that our ship intercepted."

It took a few seconds for his words to register. The memory of the night she'd finally managed to repair the ancient broadcast system long enough to send out an SOS hit her full force. How she had cried when it broke down after she sent it. Excitement and hope welled in her. "Oh, my God! You received it! It worked! You're here to rescue us! Thank you so much!"

His gaze was unflinching and steely with his reply. "Our colony was in the direct path of an ion storm. Everything has been lost."

Her jubilation was tempered by that piece of news. Hannah felt sick. "Oh, my God. We lost everything in a major quake a couple of years ago." She'd mentioned that in her SOS and immediately felt like an idiot. "But I guess you know that already."

"We need a new home, and you need help to rebuild your infrastructure." He looked over Hannah's shoulder. When she followed his gaze, she found a small group of people lingering behind her, undoubtedly drawn there by the sound of this man's ship.

"So, you want to trade resources?" Hannah asked slowly.

"Yes. We wish to reestablish our colony here, if you'll have us." He closed his eyes, as if in prayer. A moment later, more people in the same kind of suit he wore began to descend the ramp, boots echoing in near-perfect unison to their stomping.

Her hope quickly turned to ire. This wasn't the kind of help she'd envisioned for New Eden. "Wait a damn minute!"

He opened his eyes. "What?"

"You can't just take over a planet like that!"

"We will do no such thing. You said yourself that you're in need of help. Your broadcast conveyed that your infrastructure has been decimated and your population has dwindled. We can aid in your reconstruction and, perhaps, improve on it. You can direct us to arable land on which we can rebuild our society, and we will share our technology with you. Is this not an ideal solution for both of our societies?"

Hannah wasn't so sure she or anyone else on New Eden would want to make room for a group of . . . whatever the hell these people were. They lined up outside their spacecraft, their heavy flight suits molded to their bodies, and adorned with all manner of tech she had never even dreamed of, expressions blank underneath shiny black helmets. If Hannah closed her eyes and focused, she could probably hear them blink in unison. It wasn't natural, although she wasn't sure she could make that judgment based on her limited knowledge of pretty much everything in the universe. Uncanny valley, she decided. She'd read that phrase in a book with yellowing pages years ago. They seemed human, and yet not, somehow.

"Madam?" The man she'd been speaking to snapped her out of her musing. "I asked you if this is not an ideal solution to both of our societies. Will you answer?"

"What are you?" she asked. The question slipped out before she could talk herself out of it.

"We are humanoid, same as you."

"No, I mean, *what* are you? You're not human the way the rest of us on New Eden are."

"We are enhanced humanoids."

"So, like cyborgs, then."

Was it her imagination, or did a muscle tick in his jaw? It could have been a trick of the light, or lack of it. "We are what you may call cyborgs, yes."

"Do you all have the same parents or something?"

"We are a controlled society of clones, although at present, there are only one of each of us."

"Oh." She peered at a few of the faces, but none of them met her gaze, their eyes fixed on a faraway point only noticeable to them. Or maybe they were in stasis or something. "Damn."

"You have not answered my question about the mutual benefits to our societies."

"Oh, yeah." She straightened. "Well, I'll have to tell the rest of New Eden. Or what's left of it, anyway. There aren't many of us now."

"Are you not the leader?"

"No, I was out for a late-night stroll and happened to come across your spaceship. We don't have an official leader right now." She regretted the words as soon as they left her mouth. Was that a mistake to admit? New Eden was rudderless, its population of twenty-one souls just under half of what it had been before the earthquake, and completely without defenses.

Not that they'd had much in the way of defenses before the earthquake, as their planet was in the middle of nowhere, so far from trade routes that no one bothered them. The planet had been chosen for settlement by their ancestors specifically for that reason.

"You are the first person I've met," he said. "We received the SOS you transmitted. Therefore, you are the leader until you introduce us to someone with that title."

Hannah stared at him, agog. "What the fuck?"

He paused, as if considering his next words. "Perhaps we should speak with your council."

"Yeah." She looked back at the remains of the city outlined in the moonlight. There was no council, no government to speak of. "I, uh—yeah, that would make sense, except we don't have a formal council anymore. Most of them . . ." She paused, unexpected tears clogging her throat. "They didn't make it through the quake. Everyone else is the council now."

If the cyborg noticed the catch in her voice, he didn't let on. His response was as flat and emotionless as the rest of his words. "Do you need help rousing them?"

Hannah thought about how she might react if a giant cyborg hauled her out of bed and shuddered. "No, thank you. I'm pretty sure your ship woke everyone up anyway." She looked at his ship crew standing perfectly still, as if waiting for marching orders. Maybe they were.

"Where shall we wait while you notify the rest of your people?" he asked.

She looked back at the ruined city, then at the field. "I guess you could stay here." The last thing she wanted right now was their cyborg visitors to terrify the rest of the citizenry in the middle of the night.

He nodded. "We will wait for you to return."

"Okay." With another glance back at the city, she asked, "What should I call you and your people? Do I just wake everyone by telling them that there's a bunch of cyborgs waiting in the field?"

"My designation is RH103."

His response was a little jarring in its abruptness. "That's it? That's your name?"

He nodded.

"Okay. What about the rest of you?"

"We are enhanced biocybernetic organisms."

Hannah tried not to sigh in irritation. "I mean, what do you call yourselves? This is New Eden. We call ourselves New Edeners, I guess. Very creative, right? My name's Hannah Forsyth. I call myself Hannah."

Why was she babbling? What did it matter what they called themselves? She had a name for their leader; that should be enough. In fact, just having a field full of cyborgs who seemed to be willing to help rebuild New Eden should be enough.

"We are cybernetically enhanced humanoids from the former EST-213 terraformed colony."

She waited for him to continue, to tell her what they called themselves besides cyborg clones. But RH103 remained tight-lipped.

"Cyborgs, then," Hannah said.

He tilted his head, as if processing her reply.

"We'll call you cyborgs. Technology experts and Earther-descended Luddites, coexisting and rebuilding. Great." She looked back at the buildings. Candles flickered in windows with their sashes raised, and a few people had collected on the edges of the ruined street. As she suspected, it appeared that the spaceship's commotion woke everyone.

No one approached them. Irritation flared in her. What if one of the clones had pulled out a weapon and shot her? She made a mental note to sarcastically thank them for caring about her safety later.

"Do you agree that our resettling here would be ideal?" RH103 asked.

"I'll still have to run it by the rest of the people."

He pointed a gloved finger at the assembled crowd that was rapidly growing. "Is this the rest of your people?"

"Yeah, and we have a lot to discuss." She sighed. "Okay, follow me. Let's sit down and talk."

———

HANNAH HAD WORKED in an agricultural role long before the quake and kept it up now, replanting fields and trees and keeping the rest of the survivors from starving. She hated being in charge of such an important task and that she couldn't keep many of their crops from failing.

For once, their dying fields were far from her mind as she led RH103 from his ship's landing site to the amphitheater. The wrecked streets were illuminated by the others' candles and torchlight. She didn't answer many questions from the other residents, except to say, "We'll talk about it at the amphitheater, and they're here peacefully," while hoping she wasn't making a huge mistake.

Ever since New Eden's community center, where council meetings had been held, was destroyed in the earthquake, they'd been holding meetings in the amphitheater that once hosted concerts and plays. Its wooden stage was still intact, albeit sagging in parts, boards worn smooth from years of use. Its backdrop was long gone, having collapsed when Hannah was small. In front of the stage were the remains of wooden benches for the audience, now too splintered to sit on.

The amphitheater's stage was still intact, and she tried to hoist herself up to its edge. Tried, and failed, thanks to sweaty palms and her shorter-than-average height. Before she could walk to one of the sets of stairs on either side of the stage, RH103 held out his gloved hands, as if in offering. She looked at them in surprise before fixing her gaze on his face. "I can help you," he said, voice quiet.

What the hell? She hoped she wasn't making a mistake letting him touch her. If nothing else, it might reassure everyone else that he wasn't dangerous.

What was she thinking? *She* didn't know if he was dangerous yet, and she'd known him the longest.

But she let him give her a boost, lifting her as if she weighed no more than a feather. He stood next to her, hands clasped behind his back, the way she imagined a soldier would stand at attention.

She surveyed the crowd, recognizing everyone. It looked like all of New Eden's twenty-one people had gathered, perched in the remaining seats and standing on the ground in front of the stage. Candlelight and torchlight filled the amphitheater in a way that reminded her of the time before the earthquake. She thought back to a play she'd performed in as a teenager, a silly melodramatic thing with a set full of candles. Her parents had been so proud of her.

She closed her eyes, forcing the memory away. This was the worst possible time to fall into the weeds.

Surprisingly, the crowd was quiet. It had to be due to the menacing presence of the cyborg.

Hannah had no idea where to start. She cleared her throat. "This is RH103," she began.

As if her introduction unleashed the proverbial floodgates, nearly two dozen voices started to ask questions, most of which she couldn't make out. She stole a glance at RH103, whose expression remained cool and impassive in the light. This close to him, she could see his cheekbones really were as sharp as she'd thought they were when he walked off his spaceship.

"Hey! Cut it out! Let me finish!" she shouted over the din. The voices quieted enough for her to continue. "RH103 and his friends heard our distress signal." She'd sent it out over two months ago in private, not telling a soul except her best friend, Jasmine it until guilt over holding such a secret got the best of her. She'd told the others not long after, to mixed reactions.

That caught their attention. "They're here to help us rebuild?" someone called.

Were they? Hannah looked at RH103 again, but he spoke before she could.

"We are here to help," he said. "But our need for help is mutual. Our terraformed asteroid colony was in the direct path of an ion storm that forced my people to evacuate. We can help you in your recovery efforts in exchange for a place to live."

Hannah held her breath, waiting for the inevitable shitstorm at that piece of news.

When the cacophony of voices raised—some outraged, some delighted—she sighed and waited for it to die down.

Hannah's neighbor and best friend, Jasmine Sinclair, forced her way to the front of the group closest to the stage. The sight offered her a small measure of relief and regret. Jasmine was better suited to being in front of a crowd. Hell, she was better suited to being the sort of person who would run toward a mysterious flying object in the middle of the night. If she'd been there instead of

Hannah, she would have already charmed the cyborg clones into rebuilding the power grid.

Hannah beckoned for her to come closer. Candle held aloft, Jasmine did so. "I think I need your help," Hannah said into her ear.

"What for? You're doing great."

"You're better at talking to people."

"No, *you're* better at talking to people. I'm better at getting their attention." With that, Jasmine turned around to face the crowd, stuck her pinky fingers in her mouth, and released an ear-piercing whistle.

God above be praised, everyone finally fell silent.

Hannah knew the silence wouldn't last and didn't want to waste the opportunity. "We have enough space for RH103 and his friends," she said. "More than enough. And these last two years have shown that we can't rebuild things to the way they were without help. That technology doesn't exist anymore. We should embrace the help they've offered." It hadn't existed before the earthquake, either, having been established when the colony was still new, but she glossed over that. The cyborgs were bound to have something that would work for them.

"But at what cost?" The late mayor's widow, Rodelle Lansing, shuffled forward, wearing the same ragged clothes she'd donned since her husband died in the quake. Her eyes were hollow and sad, but her voice was stronger than Hannah had heard in years. She saw a flicker of the capable woman Rodelle had been before grief consumed her.

"There is none," RH103 replied. "There are twenty of us in all. We will require a suitable building to live in, perhaps one with some small apartments, since we don't require a great deal of space. If we stay on New Eden, we can't live aboard our ship long term. The fuel supplies will be exhausted keeping its functions online, and the nearest port is several days away. However, we can build housing on our own time."

There was a port only a few days away from New Eden? One with fuel? That had to mean it had other supplies too. That revelation piqued Hannah's curiosity further, and she was dying to ask RH103 more questions about life outside her planet.

"What about our infrastructure?" Rodelle asked. She stood up to her full height, something Hannah hadn't seen since her husband died. "We haven't had automatic power since the quake. We have no way of rebuilding our grid with the supplies or resources we have on hand. Can your people help with that?"

RH103 nodded. "We can. Our scans of your planetary resources indicated that there's the potential for hydroelectric energy. It's an older technology, but we can build something reliable for the planet's use."

"We already have a hydro plant that's fallen apart. Wouldn't rebuilding the solar grid be a better idea?" Hannah asked. "We have the infrastructure. It just needs to be repaired."

"The solar grid was falling apart before the quake," Jasmine reminded her. "I don't think it can be fixed. The hydro plant is more likely to be salvageable."

"How long would it take before the hydroelectric plant is operational?" Hannah asked.

"We would have to conduct a survey and compare our resources. We could have a definitive answer for you within two days," RH103 replied.

"Two days?" Hannah was incredulous. Forgetting that she had an audience, she faced him, eyes wide. "How the hell can you complete that kind of survey in two days?"

"They're cyborgs," Jasmine muttered.

"I know. But that still seems incredible and unrealistic."

"Perhaps for you," RH103 said coolly. "But this is within our capabilities."

It had to be, didn't it? They could travel around space, unimpeded by gravity or normal human functions. If they could complete a survey in days, then hopefully, it wouldn't be beyond their capabilities to build a power grid in a matter of weeks.

Hannah took a shaky breath and stole a glance at RH103's impassive face.

Something flickered in his expression. Hope, maybe? He wanted a place to live as badly as she wanted to see hers rebuilt. Yet she had the feeling, if she asked, he would leave New Eden behind and never return.

Where else would they go? Though New Eden had been decimated in the quake, his home had been obliterated off the star charts.

"Let's take a vote," she announced. "A show of hands. Who thinks the cyborgs should be allowed to stay and help us rebuild?"

"This is irregular," Rodelle said, but her voice wavered. She was as tired of living in the dark as everyone else, tired of hand pumping funny-tasting water, tired of a meager diet and going hungry.

"On a conditional basis," Jasmine said. A murmur of voices agreed.

"We shall work out any conditions in the morning," RH103 said. "All of you are tired and overwhelmed. Why don't we reconvene here at eleven hundred hours? I will return to my ship for the rest of the night and bring my fellow cyborgs in the morning. You have my word that we will not leave our ship until that time."

Hannah met the gazes of Rodelle and Jasmine.

Jasmine gave her a smile and a hopeful look, and Rodelle, the barest of nods.

"All right," she said. "Let's meet back here tomorrow morning." She hoisted herself off the stage. "Show's over, folks. Let's get back to bed."

CHAPTER TWO

RH103 and the rest of his brethren hadn't needed to listen to New Eden's SOS broadcast to know that their planet had experienced devastation. Their cruiser's sensors had told them as much—that it was a broken place with a smaller than expected population, considering how long the colony had been there.

Yet the condition of the planet's ruined city and its citizenry's despair had surprised him. He, like everyone else of his kind, had never encountered a place or people so broken. If RH103 had been capable of being shaken to his core, he would have experienced it when he looked at Hannah Forsyth or the people who looked up to her.

She didn't consider herself a leader, but the residents did. So did RH103. Only a leader would run across a field in the middle of the night to greet a strange ship that had broken her planet's atmosphere instead of running for help. Only a leader would send out the impassioned plea for help across the galaxy, as she had.

A leader or a fool. He hoped it was the former.

They have agreed to let us stay?

His fellow cyborgs' collective voice filled his head, a familiar and usually welcome buzzing sensation. He had switched off his brain's broadcast signal while in the destroyed outdoor theater, not wanting to appear distracted if the other cyborgs asked him questions. He'd noticed the strange look that crossed Hannah's face when they spoke to him after they landed. They'd asked about whether they would have to stay in their pods in the cruiser for the night or if accommodations would be provided.

Yes, for now, he replied. *We must stay on the cruiser for the night. We will speak with the residents in the morning, after they've had some rest.* Staying in the cruiser indefinitely was not an option, given the fuel it would waste maintaining the ship's functions. They needed to conserve it for an inevitable off-world supply run in the near future.

In the moment when Hannah Forsyth met him in the field, her obvious feelings of curiosity and terror warring on her face, he had never been more grateful for insisting that the entire collective read about expected etiquette and manners in organic societies. Their original plan had been to land and start rebuilding immediately, heedless of the time, and RH103 was very glad he looked into other organic humanoid cultures before implementing it.

They have no suitable place for our cruiser. A field is not appropriate for long-term storage, said CW44. *There's no fuel, no protection from the elements, nothing..*

You saw its scans, RH103 replied. *Their landing pad was destroyed before the earthquake happened. This is not a culture that places high value on interplanetary travel.*

Or any kind of travel, for that matter. There was no need to, when New Eden had everything they needed to survive in one place. They'd built their city on the one habitable land mass, in the south, where it was warmest. The northern part was uninhabited and largely composed of mountainous territory and caves, with nowhere to plant crops or build infrastructure. The city was surrounded by freshwater oceans, a rarity in this part of the galaxy. New Eden's climate was pleasant to unenhanced bodies, the land in the south arable, the air and water suitable for human life. Or would be, if its infrastructure was repaired.

We shall find an appropriate place for our cruiser at a later time, RH103 replied. He strode across the field, where his brethren still waited outside the ship in a perfectly formed straight line. Their backs were ramrod straight, eyes trained ahead. Their black helmets shone under the light offered by the twin moons overhead. For the first time, he understood how they could be seen as intimidating.

Back aboard, he commanded them. *Into the pods for the night.*

If they'd been capable of groaning over their shared broadcast link, he was sure they would have. He didn't blame them. While he didn't mind the recharging pods, some of the others found them uncomfortable. As it was, they walked back up the cruiser's ramp, single file, with RH103 at the rear.

———

DESPITE THE EXHAUSTION pulling at her, Hannah knew she wouldn't sleep well, if at all. It took over an hour for her to get back to her house as the remains of New Eden's citizenry peppered her with questions.

How many others were there? How big was the space-ship? Was she *sure* the cyborgs were there to help them? Why had she been out so late at night, picking vegetables?

Hannah answered as best as she could, glossing over the queries about collecting produce in the middle of the night. She caught sympathetic glances from Jasmine, who knew about her sleep issues since the quake and how she dealt with them. How did one tell her friends and acquaintances that their agriculture production was so far behind that she had to harvest in the middle of the night, just to keep the city fed? Just to keep their food from rotting in the fields?

The thought of the tomato plants she'd left behind that needed to be picked and distributed made her heart hurt. But she could hardly steal back out of her house at this late hour, with most of the city wide awake, to pick them. She told herself that it would be okay, that an extra day or two on the vine wouldn't spoil them. That her inaction wouldn't doom the rest of the New Edeners to starvation.

When she reached her house, Jasmine quickly followed her to the front door and grabbed her elbow. "Do you want me to stay with you?" she said, voice quiet. Hannah had to strain to hear her over the voices of the people who had tagged along for the rest of the walk home.

Hannah considered Jasmine's question for a moment. It would feel so good to talk to her, to unload her fears about New Eden's future, her grief, the planet's collective grief. And that was without even touching on the cyborgs she had invited to live with them.

But talking would take too much of her precious energy. "Thank you, but I think I'll be okay for the night," Hannah murmured.

Jasmine nodded.

"You'll be at the amphitheater tomorrow, right?"

"Of course." Jasmine looked affronted at the very hint of her not being in attendance. "I'm curious to see what a gang of cyborg clones looks like. I wonder if they're all as huge as the one you marched through the streets."

"I did not . . ." Hannah sighed. "I did not *march* him. I don't think that's even possible." She thought of how

RH103 had loomed over her, making her feel small. Yet he had listened to her, even helped haul her up to the stage.

The memory of his hands on her shouldn't have sent a shiver through her, but it did. And it wasn't one of fear.

Jasmine noticed. "Are you all right?"

"Are you serious?"

"I mean, less all right than usual."

Hannah shook her head. "Yeah. I'll be fine. I just need some sleep."

"You're *sure* you don't want me to stay with you? It'll be a sleepover, like when we were kids."

It would be like the early days after the earthquake, too, when neither of them could bear to be alone. Hannah didn't want to live that again. Forcing a smile to her face, she said, "I appreciate it, Jas, I really do. But I need some rest and time to think."

"Got it." Jasmine wrapped her in a fierce hug. "If you change your mind, you know where I am. I'll see you in the morning."

As she suspected she would, Hannah grabbed only a few snatches of sleep in between worrying. She gave up trying to rest when the sun's rays peeked through her bedroom window. She quickly washed and dressed, determined to get started on the tomato picking before the meeting with the cyborgs.

The fields were a fifteen-minute walk from her house, something that she usually enjoyed because the city's destruction wasn't as evident on her route. But the sight of a group of giant, black-clad men already at work, pulling at the plants, shattered her calm.

Rage and frustration bubbled in her, bringing tears to her eyes. "Hey!" she shouted, and picked up her pace into a run. "What the hell do you think you're doing?"

They moved with rapid, soulless motions, plucking

tomatoes and other vegetables with machine-like precision. She saw her months of hard work evaporate as they dropped them into the baskets that they must have pilfered from the supply shed, taking New Eden's meager resources for their own.

"Hey!" she yelled again as she reached the field. She halted, trying to catch her breath. She brushed away angry tears with the back of her hand, hating that she cried when she was furious. "What's this?"

A cyborg raised his head, fixing eyes that were an inhuman shade of green on her. "RH103 ordered us here."

RH103 did this? The revelation made her heart hurt, though she couldn't say why. Hannah hated that she had let herself trust him. "Why would he do that?"

The cyborg looked at her like she was crazy. "He said you were in obvious need of help with your crops. They're going to die if they aren't harvested soon."

Shock had her frozen in place. It took a few seconds for his words to sink in. "He noticed that?" Now Hannah felt like crying for another reason.

The cyborg nodded solemnly. Without looking at his hands, he resumed picking. "After we scanned your planet last night, he said that many of the cultivated crops are in danger of spoiling."

"Yeah. That's why I'm here." Her pent-up frustration and anger leached out of her, leaving her feeling deflated and exhausted all over again.

He tilted his head in confusion. "Why are you crying? We thought you were in need of help."

"You have no idea." Heaving an embarrassed sigh, she walked through the rows of planted vegetables until she was beside the cyborg and started picking tomatoes. "I'm sorry, I didn't mean to bite your head off."

"You did no such thing."

"I meant figuratively."

He blinked, as if contemplating her words, but didn't respond.

"Thank you," she added. "I do appreciate this. I just wasn't expecting you to dive in first thing in the morning."

"Do you not have people who can harvest?"

"I do, but there aren't enough. And we're not even touching on the subject of other agricultural production. We're severely lacking in protein-based foods right now, for instance."

"I didn't see any meat supplies."

"Meat supplies" was an odd term, but Hannah didn't push it. "Most of the animals died in the earthquake," she replied. "The chickens we still have are mostly off-limits, since we depend on their eggs."

"We could clone the chickens," the cyborg said nonchalantly. He moved a meter away to the next tomato plant and pulled off the ripened ones.

He spoke of it as casually as if it was nothing more unusual than a sunny day. Incredulity wound through her. "You could do that?"

"We clone ourselves with great success. Cloning livestock is well within our abilities."

"Wow," Hannah said, surprised. But why was she? Of course, they could clone animals. "Thank you."

"RH103 said we must collaborate. Your people can provide the DNA, and we can replicate it."

"Do you mean people too? Because I don't think the people of New Eden will go for cloning ourselves."

The cyborg faced her, paused, and his expression went blank. Hannah froze. Had she short-circuited his head somehow?

But a few seconds later, he blinked. "RH103 agrees with you."

"What?" She looked around the field for RH103. "Where is he?"

"Aboard our cruiser, making reports for your community meeting later this morning."

"He was *listening* to us?"

"Everyone is listening to us."

Hannah had suspected that they had some kind of common broadcast link, but she hadn't expected that it was so closely connected. "Do you have a hive mind or something?"

"We share information and conversations freely."

"What are you called, or is RH103 the only person who has his own name?"

"My designation is SP29."

"Nice to meet you. I guess you already know I'm Hannah."

The cyborg nodded. "You're the leader of New Eden."

"I'm really not."

"Your voice is the one on the SOS broadcast."

Hannah didn't want to think about when she'd made that desperate plea on New Eden's ruined equipment. "I did. There was no one else to do that."

"Then you are the interim leader of New Eden, until your people hold an election."

It was on the tip of Hannah's tongue to point out that there weren't enough people left to bother holding an election, but she refrained from doing so. She didn't have the energy to get into such a discussion, not when she would be taking the stage again in a couple of hours.

She turned back to the tomatoes and resumed picking them.

———

IT TOOK RH103 a few moments to put a name to what he felt as he approached New Eden's ruined amphitheater.

He was *nervous*.

He was scared that New Eden would reject him and his brethren, force them back aboard their cruiser and back out into the open bleakness of deep space. There was nothing left for them out there since their world was destroyed.

By sending some of his brothers out to help, to show that they would be worthy new citizens, he may well have jeopardized their chances of acceptance. SP29 had told him of Hannah's distress via their shared broadcast link at seeing some of them harvesting vegetables that were in dire need of being picked. She'd thought they were trying to conquer New Eden, take their resources.

RH103 had fucked it up.

Hannah arrived at the amphitheater a few minutes early, as he had, a trail of cyborgs behind her. RH103 could smell the soil on them as they approached and noticed a streak of dirt across Hannah's forehead under the brim of her large woven sunhat. Dark half-moons under her eyes revealed her sleepless night, undoubtedly one of many since the disaster had struck the planet.

She looked up at him in surprise. "Where's your helmet?"

RH103's heart skipped a beat at her question, and he made a mental note to run a full diagnostic later. *She noticed I changed my appearance!* "I thought it would be prudent to appear less machine-like," he replied. "So, I removed it."

Before he could send a suggestion to the rest of the cyborgs to do the same, everyone started to take off theirs as well.

"Huh." Hannah regarded him thoughtfully under her hat's brim. "You have nice hair."

SP29's voice filled his mind. *Are you malfunctioning? Your pulse is elevated.*

I'm fine, RH103 replied. *It's nothing.*

But it wasn't. He'd never received compliments on his appearance before. He found he liked them.

"Thank you for sending help today," she added. "That means a lot to me. To all of us." She inclined her head toward where the amphitheater was filling up with her people.

She looked like she wanted to say more, perhaps about her initial reaction to the cyborgs, but she looked over the assembling crowd instead. "Let's get started," she said quietly and jumped up on the edge of the stage without waiting for him to offer his help. He did likewise, albeit more easily.

She took off her hat to better see everyone. For the first time, RH103 saw how her braided, sun-bleached brown hair shone in the late morning light, a sharp contrast to his shorter and more practical style. Her skin was deeply tanned, unlike his, which had hardly been touched by sunlight. Remembering that she'd noticed his hair, he felt warm all over again.

RH103?

There was SP29 again, his internal voice curious. RH103 shut down his internal link, to better protect his thoughts and physical reactions.

The crowd was more subdued this morning, and he wondered if any of them had slept since the excitement a few hours earlier. He remained quiet, letting Hannah start the meeting.

"So, I think everyone knows about our new room-mates," she began.

Roommates? That sounded promising. Why did it sound promising?

"They've been forthcoming about what they're able to offer in exchange for living here," she continued. "I woke up this morning and found some of them harvesting food, which is a huge job that I've been dealing with mostly on my own."

A murmur rippled through the crowd. Evidently, working under the sun was unpopular.

"I've also been informed that our new friends have the ability to clone livestock," she said. "We all know that we've been short of protein-rich foods, and this technology could help us get back to better diets. And there's other technology too." She looked at RH103, dark brown eyes wide. "We should've sat down to talk about that," she muttered, quiet enough so only he could hear.

RH103 stepped forward. "We can help rebuild your infrastructure," he announced.

"How long would that take?" someone in the crowd asked.

That was an encouraging sign. "We would have to make a full assessment of all the damage," he replied.

"We have no power," the same voice said. "We haven't for two years. No running water in a lot of the houses anymore, either. Not all of them have pumps."

"It's bad," said Hannah quietly. "And we're short of people who know how to do things like keep a power station running."

"We can do that," RH103 said. Louder, to the rest of the town, he said, "Our people started from scratch many years ago. It took less than eighty days to build a colony on a terraformed planet. This will certainly be faster, especially since the planet is already habitable." He looked down at his fellow cyborgs, lined up in front of the stage, as if they were a military unit of old. "We will need places to live. We cannot stay in our cruiser permanently."

A young woman stepped forward, about the same age as Hannah. RH103 remembered them speaking the night before at the amphitheater. Her white-blond hair was held back from her face with a pair of metal combs lightly tinged with rust. "There are empty houses available," she said, voice wavering.

RH103 understood why they were empty.

"Some of them are sound, and others will need to be repaired," the woman added. "I don't see why you couldn't live in them."

That comment earned another wave of discussion, with some people opposed to the idea. Hannah looked at them as their voices rose, then at RH103.

"Not in my uncle's house!" someone shouted. "That was *his* house!"

Hannah pinched the bridge of her nose between her fingers. "I'm doing this all wrong," she muttered.

"There was bound to be some dissent," RH103 replied.

"You're right. You need somewhere to live, and we have some places available, although not enough for all of you to have your own house."

"We don't mind living communally."

"The number of vacant houses that are actually safe to live in is very few. I think some of you will either be living with us or will have to stay on the cruiser. I don't know." She clapped her hands and then, louder, said, "Okay, let's talk about this!"

"I don't want strangers in my house!" The same man who had spoken about not wanting cyborgs in his late uncle's home gave pointed looks to them now.

"Then you don't have to," Hannah said tiredly. "Ollie,

you don't have enough room for someone else, anyway. Anyone who has a spare bedroom and doesn't mind a new roommate, please raise your hand."

"Does that count you?" the man she called Ollie countered. "You're still living in a family home."

"My family's home that they built when they originally settled here," Hannah shot back. "And of course, that counts me." She raised her hand, then glared defiantly at the crowd.

The blonde woman raised hers as well. Slowly, other hands lifted.

A knot of tension that RH103 hadn't realized he'd been holding in his shoulders loosened. Based on the number of people willing to let out rooms in their homes, in addition to the few empty houses available, his brethren wouldn't have to live aboard the cruiser indefinitely. Their fuel reserves were safe for now.

"I have a spare bedroom," Hannah said. "I can offer space to one person."

SP29 stepped forward and turned around to face her. He opened his mouth to speak.

A flash of jealousy—unexpected and unfamiliar—rose in RH103 like hot bile in his throat. The very thought of his fellow cyborg, someone he'd always considered a friend, living with her made him want to throttle him.

What in the galaxy's name is wrong with me?

"I could stay with you," RH103 said to Hannah, voice low.

SP29 resumed his position in front of the stage.

Hannah looked at him in surprise and slowly lowered her hand. "Okay," she said. She plunked her hat back on, its brim flopping a little over an eye. "Why don't you get your stuff, and I'll take you home?"

CHAPTER THREE

Of course, it hadn't been as simple as RH103 grabbing his things from the spaceship still resting in the field. They stayed behind at the amphitheater, helping to assign billets, while Hannah spoke to the people restoring empty houses to figure out how many cyborgs could be put up in them.

By early afternoon, housing had been decided for all twenty cyborgs, and only she and RH103 were left in the amphitheater.

"I think that went better than expected," Hannah said, barely suppressing a yawn.

"Were you expecting more opposition?"

"Yes. And I don't think the worst of our growing pains is over yet." She looked at the rows of empty stone benches in the audience, at the scrubby grass growing between them. "Do you need any help getting your things from your ship?"

"I don't have much in the way of personal belongings, but perhaps we have some tech on board that will be useful in your home. Do you want to take a look?"

She had never been aboard a spaceship before. Curiosity had her asking, "Why not?" She fell into step with RH103. His stride was longer than hers, but she forced herself to keep up. "Although I doubt I'll know much about your toys. We don't use a lot of that sort of thing here."

"We noticed that, and all of us have questions as to why."

"Our ancestors settled here for the purpose of getting away from all of that." She adjusted her hat brim against the light of the twin suns blazing in the sky. "I think a lot of us are resentful over that decision, for obvious reasons. We really needed help the last couple of years."

RH103 slowed down to match her pace. "Why would your predecessors do such a thing?"

"We'll have plenty of time to talk about how our great-great-great-whatever grandparents screwed us over, roomie." A dirt road led away from the amphitheater to the edge of the city where the spaceship had landed. Puffs of dust swirled around their ankles, marring the shiny finish on RH103's black boots.

Roomie. She couldn't believe she had agreed to such a thing.

Nor could she quite process RH103's eagerness to live with her. Maybe it was because she was the only person he had spoken to so far. She was as close to familiar as he could get on New Eden.

At least this would mean she would learn more about the cyborg clone society from their leader himself. If nothing else, their sharing her house—her parents' house —could make both of their jobs a little easier.

The spaceship's exterior door was closed when they arrived, the ramp gone. This close to the ship, Hannah felt a little intimidated. But it quickly gave way to curiosity when RH103 stripped off one of his gloves and pressed his hand into a white screen next to the door. A buzzing sounded before the door cycled open and the ramp extended.

RH103 replaced his glove. "Follow me."

Heart pounding in uncharacteristic excitement, Hannah did so.

It took a few seconds for her vision to adjust to the interior's harsh yellow light. It was the only color that she could see. Everything else was dull gray metal panels and decking, broken up by the occasional flashing light. It was far more sterile and boring than Hannah had expected. "Where's your room?" she asked.

"I have none."

"Where do you sleep?"

RH103 nodded toward a corridor and started to walk. Hannah followed him, noting screens inset into the walls that flared to life when he strode past them. She was dying to ask what information scrolled across them, to find out what New Eden had been missing over the last few generations, but was distracted when RH103 halted. He held out his hand in an oddly grand gesture, revealing rows of coffin-sized closets on either side of the narrow room. As it was, she and RH103 could barely stand side by side, given the close quarters.

He turned to the one closest to him on his right side. "This pod is mine."

"How do you live in that?"

"I don't. I merely rest here."

Hannah stared at it, agog. "How?"

"This is where we rest and download reports and scans. We interface with the cruiser and each other."

"No, I mean, how do you sleep standing up? With all these wires plugged into you?" She reached into the pod and picked up a thin red cable. "And wouldn't you go nuts listening to all your friends talking to you telepathically?"

"It isn't sleeping so much as recharging."

That made sense, given that he was probably half-machine, at this point. "How will you take to sleeping in a bed? No one has any pods in their houses. We don't even have power yet."

RH103 gave the barest of shrugs. "We're capable of sleeping the way organic humans do. We can still communicate with each other via our broadcast link. Or I could walk to another house, knock on the door, and speak to someone." He reached into the pod, his arm brushing against Hannah's, sending unexpected sparks across her bare skin.

That was weird. She pulled away, hoping he didn't notice her flush.

He pressed a button inset in the wall that she hadn't noticed before. A drawer popped out, and he removed a duffel bag from it, slinging it over his shoulder. "I have my things," he announced.

She shouldn't have been surprised, yet she was. "That's it?"

He nodded. "I have two changes of clothes and some hygiene items."

"Wow. You pack light."

The look he gave her was inscrutable, and she wondered if she'd said something wrong.

"I have some other things I'd like to bring," he continued. "We have universal batteries to share with you."

"You mean mobile power sources?" Excitement welled in her at the idea of again having lights that didn't come from tree sap candles.

"Yes, and they can recharge power sources too. Everyone living with a human was told to bring one."

"That's a hell of a hostess gift," Hannah replied. "Better than a bottle of wine or bouquet these days."

He led her down the corridor, farther into the belly of the ship. "Are these types of gifts typical on this planet?"

"This one, and I'm sure others with Earther-descended cultures. I haven't met any others." Lights flared to life as RH103 strode beneath them and she looked at them, fascinated, until they reached a closed door at the corridor's end. RH103 stood before it until a slim beam of red light scanned his eye. Something whirred, and the door opened.

Hannah looked around him to see a small room, brightly illuminated by a glowing yellow-white panel in the ceiling. It was stacked with weapons and gadgets that looked like the things she'd seen in the yellowing comic books she'd read as a child.

As though he could read her mind, RH103 said, "This is one of our weapons lockers."

Mild alarm flared through her. "Are the batteries weapons?"

Just as quickly, it was gone with his response. "No, but they can recharge weapons, so we keep them together." He picked up a nondescript-looking gray cube and held it out to her.

She gingerly accepted it, turning it over in her hands. It fit neatly into her palm and weighed about the same as a ripe tomato, surprisingly heavy for something so small. Tiny pinpricks of green light glowed along its surface on all sides. Ports were inset into one side, and she guessed they were for cables. "How long does it last?" she asked.

"They can provide ten thousand hours of service before being recharged. We have recharge banks on the cruiser, but they can also be charged in sunlight."

Hannah stared at the small device, gobsmacked. "We definitely have an overabundance of sunlight here. This is like something out of a children's story. The poor people on a wrecked planet in the middle of nowhere get rescued by visitors who have tech that charges itself in the sun. This is crazy."

"I believe we're offering each other rescue. Our home was destroyed, and you have generously provided us with a new place to live."

"We still have a lot of details to work out about that, by the way."

"Of course."

At least they were on the same page. Hannah looked behind him at the weapons. "How often do you get into fights? Why do you need all that?"

"Some parts of the galaxy are less savory than others, and there are those who could try to steal our tech. We keep ourselves prepared for anything."

Hannah hadn't thought about that, and she felt like an idiot. "RH103?" It felt weird not calling him by a normal name.

"Yes?" His voice was curious, as if he hadn't just revealed that he and his cyborg friends had to keep themselves armed to the teeth to survive.

"Is New Eden going to be invaded by people who want your cybernetic arms?"

"My arms are organic with cybernetic enhancements."

"You're being obtuse." Why the hell hadn't she thought of that? Had her inviting the cyborgs to live with them possibly exposed her people to war?

"I'm not." RH103 sounded genuinely confused at the terse note in her voice.

"Are there people after you now? What are the odds

that we're going to be blown out of the galaxy because of what you are? Are there bounty hunters after you?"

"Oh." Understanding dawned on RH103's face. "No. No one has tried to steal our tech in our current collective memory. When we traded with others, it was with peaceful people. There are no known threats against us." He unsealed his duffel, picked up another battery, and deposited it inside.

"Do you need anything else?"

He shook his head. "I have everything."

They walked through the spaceship back to its airlock, where the exterior door was still open. Hannah adjusted her hat's brim against the sunlight, the battery clutched tightly in her hand.

After two years of darkness and cold food, she and the rest of New Eden could finally start to rebuild their lives. She could eat dinner with the kitchen light on again, read a book at night without her eyes straining, if and when she ever had the concentration to do such a thing again.

"How many of you are there?"

"Twenty in all," he replied.

"You're clones," she said. "How does that work? Are you going to keep cloning yourselves now that you're here?"

"How else would we reproduce?"

His voice was deadpan as usual, but something about the innocence in his question, combined with her exhaustion and anxiety, struck her as wildly funny. She stopped dead in her tracks and couldn't stop giggling.

It took only a few seconds before RH103 said, "Oh, I see."

When she was able to compose herself, she asked, "Are you still planning on spawning yourselves in tanks?"

"It's a little more nuanced than that, and we haven't

considered it. I think we might be getting ahead of ourselves."

"But seriously, you *do* spawn in incubators or something, right?"

He nodded. "I'm the one hundredth and third clone of my original organic parent."

Hannah nearly stumbled over a stone at that revelation. "One hundred and fucking *three*? I'm never going to stop being surprised by you, am I?"

"I'm sure you have many surprises in store for me."

"Yeah, probably, but I think it'll be easier for you to wrap your head around sleeping in a bed every night than it was for me to find out that you're the hundred and third copy of a person. Our ancestors came here to escape from that kind of thing."

He was quiet for a few seconds. "Do you disapprove of it?"

For some reason she couldn't determine, Hannah felt like her answer was important to him. She was honest. "I resent that they deliberately took steps to cut us off from the galaxy for their own selfish and shortsighted reasons. We've lost out on advances in medicine and technology. I had a hell of a time reassembling the equipment in the old launch tower to send out an SOS. If we'd had a warning system in place, maybe we could have reduced the mortality rate in the quake."

"I meant about our reproduction methods."

"Oh!" She felt like an idiot. "No, no concerns from me on that front. I'm glad you're here and you have your tech. We need to be able to protect ourselves against future quakes."

That was what rankled her the most, making her curse generations of long-dead Forsyths to whatever hell they currently roasted in. New Eden had a history of minor tremors, occurring once every year or so since the planet was originally colonized.

"It sounds like you need seismograph technology," RH103 surmised.

"Yeah."

"Creating such a device is within our capabilities."

Tears sprang to Hannah's eyes, and she impatiently brushed them away. She thought about her parents and so many others, dead in the quake after the community center collapsed. "You could really do that?"

"It's fairly straightforward. We will have to sit down soon and sort out which infrastructure needs to be replaced or created first. I think seismographs are as important as clean water in a place like this." He stopped walking, dust swirling around their feet. "Why are you crying?"

"You weren't supposed to see that." She sniffled and pasted a smile to her face. "It's nothing. Well, not exactly." She tried again. "Everything that you take for granted as normal—that's what is going to save us. It feels too good to be true." A sob escaped her. "I'm sorry, I didn't plan on breaking down today."

"Hannah."

His voice was uncharacteristically soft, more human than she had heard from him before. She looked up, her gaze meeting his.

Dark eyes searched her face, as if he couldn't read her expression. Maybe he couldn't. "You sent out the SOS, didn't you?"

She nodded.

"You saved your people," he said. "You also saved mine. You're doing enough."

It was the first time Hannah had ever heard or thought such a thing. If they weren't in public, she would have broken down and cried, letting out her grief and relief physically.

But they were in public, and she couldn't deal with anyone passing by asking her what was wrong. "Thank you," she said and gave him a watery smile. "Let's go home."

CHAPTER FOUR

ONCE UPON A TIME, Hannah's house would have looked homey and inviting, even to a cyborg unaccustomed to such sights. Like the other houses in Hannah's neighborhood, hers was made of wood and yellow-colored stone native to New Eden. It was probably sourced from the old quarry on the east side of the landmass the ship had detected when it broke atmosphere. Wooden shingles of varying colors and ages from years of repair formed the roof. Stumps revealed where trees had once grown and the remaining grass was patchy. The small house now looked forlorn, a couple of its windows replaced with wooden boards—one more casualty in the natural disaster that had rocked the planet. Hannah flushed when she looked at it, then at RH103, and he thought she might be embarrassed about its condition.

But why would she be? She had spent the last two years trying to keep her people alive any way she could. She hadn't mentioned who she had lost close to her in the quake, but he knew she'd experienced significant loss and hadn't had a chance to grieve it.

She opened the door and held it for him. "There isn't much. But I have an extra bedroom for you to use."

He stepped into a small foyer, its walls papered with a cheerful flower print that had faded over the decades, peeling in some places. The wooden floor creaked comfortably beneath their weight, buffered by a handmade rag rug in a rainbow pattern. To their right was the kitchen, sunlight streaming across the floorboards from its intact window. To their left was a lounge area, darkened due to the wooden board covering the window where the glass used to be. A few framed holographs of people who looked like Hannah were affixed to the walls, happy scenes frozen in time. Other pictures were drawn on rough paper with charcoal, probably created after their holography tech failed or they ran out of supplies to keep it going.

A scrap of an old memory that wasn't truly his flashed in his mind. He saw through floor-to-ceiling glass windows at a storm raging outside. When he looked down, he saw he was hundreds of meters up, looking down at a gray city, its buildings running the gamut from old and rundown to modern and luxurious. The feel of thick carpet pile beneath his bare feet told him he was in a unit that was in the latter category.

RH103 shook his head. It had been a long time since his subconscious had dredged up a memory of the original Rhys Hammond.

"RH103?" Hannah's voice brought him back to the present. "The bedrooms are upstairs." She inclined her head at a flight of stairs, covered with a threadbare carpet runner.

He followed her. A bathroom was directly ahead of them at the landing, and a bedroom was on either side of it. She pushed open the door to the left. "Here you are. It isn't a recharging coffin, but I hope it'll be okay for now."

While clean, the bedroom had clearly been unused for a long time. The window was covered with sheer blue drapes that matched the blue covers on the wide bed, its mattress sagging in the middle. Striped paper covered the walls, peeling a little at the corners, and there were more framed charcoal portraits here, these clearly of Hannah as a small child with two people he assumed were her parents. This had been Hannah's parents' bedroom, a place she'd lovingly kept intact.

"Will this be okay?" she asked.

As if it would be anything but. "Of course." He tried to smile, but the gesture didn't come easily to him. "Thank you."

"I don't have automatic running water right now," she said. "None of the houses do. There are manual pumps and drains on all the bathroom fixtures and the kitchen sink. All the water is cold, though. We have no way to heat it up."

Not for long, if RH103 had anything to say about it. The first thing he would see to was the restoration of New Eden's power grid. "Where is your hydroelectric station?" he asked.

She blinked in surprise. "You're going to start on that now?"

"Of course. A reliable power source and hot water are essential for survival."

"It's on the westernmost edge of the city, the big brown building. Halfway between the waterfalls and the old solar grid. You can't miss it. It's mostly intact."

RH103 closed his eyes and sent out a short message to his fellow cyborgs. *Everyone who hasn't found a detail to work on will meet me at the power station in thirty minutes.*

A chorus of affirmatives flooded his head in response, eight in all.

"Were you talking to your friends?" Hannah asked.

He nodded. "We're going to start those repairs immediately."

She looked like she was going to cry again, but when she spoke, her voice was steady. "Wow. Thank you. Some of us tried to repair it after the quake, but everyone who was familiar with the tech had passed away. We stopped trying to fix it, because we were worried about burning everything down or electrocuting ourselves."

"A wise decision."

"It's hydro powered," Hannah added. "If that helps."

"I'm certain this is within our capabilities."

Her face crumpled for a second, and she looked away at the closed door across the small hallway that presumably led to her bedroom. "This seems too good to be true," she muttered.

She had already said as much, and RH103 wondered how long it would be before she understood that their streak of misfortune and grief might be finally coming to an end. "Hannah."

Her shoulders raised as she took a deep breath. Without turning around, she said, "Yeah?"

"I promised you that we could return your planet to a state of normalcy. I meant that. Eight of us are going to the power station, and we'll have a workable plan and timeline of repairs by the end of the day, I promise."

"Unbelievable." At last, she faced him. "If you're settled in and ready to go to the power station, I'm going back to the fields."

"I will see you this evening, then."

"I'll make dinner. You *do* eat regular food, right?"

"Our organics require it."

"I hope you like eggs."

Another old memory popped into his head—sitting in

an air-conditioned white-walled restaurant, sunlight flooding the space. In front of him was an oversized white plate. Fruit and slices of toast, topped with white blobs, were artfully arranged on it. The scent of hot coffee reached his nostrils.

RH103 hadn't had the blobs he knew as poached eggs, but he knew what they were. Rhys Hammond had liked them. "I think I do," RH103 replied.

"I'm going to hold you to that," she said. "I'll be back here around six-thirty tonight." Gripping the banister, she descended the stairs. "Don't fry your circuits while you're at the power station. Our medical facilities are somewhat lacking for people with cybernetic hearts."

"My heart is mostly organic."

"Yeah, we're missing the personnel to fix those too. Stay safe, okay?" From the bottom of the stairs, she turned beseeching eyes to him.

She cared about his wellbeing, and that of his fellow cyborgs. While RH103 wasn't great at reading the facial expressions of strictly organic humanoids yet, he could understand Hannah's well enough to know that it was personal. She wasn't only concerned about his ability to restore their power.

He liked having someone be concerned about him. "I will," he promised.

"There's water at the station, but it isn't potable," she added. She thumbed in the kitchen's direction. "Take a water bottle with you. My kitchen pump works fine, and the water tastes funny, but it won't kill you."

RH103's programming would eliminate any parasites or bacteria present in dirty water, but he didn't say that. He hated that she would have had to drink the water to know if it was safe. "Thank you, I will."

She adjusted her sunhat. "See you tonight, RH103."

"See you," he said, echoing her farewell as she left the house.

As he walked down the stairs, taking in the pictures of a happier Hannah and her family in better days, he thought about how his numerical designation had never bothered him until now. He'd never spent time with organic people; none of his previous clones had, except for the original Rhys Hammond, scant as his memories of him were.

He found a battered tin water bottle in the kitchen and filled it at the pump, its chill pleasant through his gloved hands. When he left the house, stepping into the bright summer sunshine, he wondered if it wasn't time to take on a regular human name now that he lived among them.

THE SAME GROUP of cyborgs that Hannah met earlier in the day were back at the fields, harvesting food with their same remarkable speed. SP29 stood up from where he was crouching when she approached the field and saluted her, a smile on his face.

She'd never seen a cyborg smile so easily. God knew it didn't come easy to RH103. She wasn't sure how to react to it or the salute, so she said what she would have to a regular human: "At ease, soldier."

"Welcome back," SP29 said when she took a position at a tomato plant. "We're on track to have everything harvested that needs to be done within the next two days."

Stunned, Hannah's hand hovered over a ripe tomato. "Are you fucking serious?"

"Of course. We also noticed the canning supplies in the barn over there. It *is* a barn, isn't it?" SP29 pointed to the structure that held the remains of New Eden's livestock. It was a small structure, the only one that could be repaired after the larger, main barn fell to pieces in the quake, taking all of New Eden's cows and most of its chickens with it.

"It's a pretty pathetic excuse for a barn, but yeah, that's it."

"Your chickens are in good health, by the way. We checked."

"Thank you."

"The building itself could use some reinforcements."

"I'm not surprised. We were in a hurry to fix it after the earthquake."

SP29 nodded. "I see. Well, we can certainly help with the foundation repairs."

The barn didn't have much of a foundation to begin with, so anything they could do would be helpful. "Thank you."

"Thank *you* for your hospitality," SP29 replied, then he changed the subject. "I've found a room in a house with Jasmine. She said she's your friend?"

"My best friend, yeah." Not that they had spent much time together since the quake. Hannah didn't have the wherewithal to be a good friend in these times.

But Jasmine had still always been there for her, waiting until she was ready to talk. Hannah wondered if that day would ever come.

As if SP29 understood that Hannah didn't want to talk about her social relationships, he steered the conversation back to agriculture. "Would you like us to start canning tomatoes, or would you prefer we start harvesting potatoes or apples? We noticed the crops have come in."

"Canning," Hannah replied. "I'm so behind on all of that, and I don't want these tomatoes to go to waste any more than they already have. I'll show you our setup."

SP29 closed his eyes for a couple of seconds, and the rest of the cyborgs stood up, then followed him and Hannah to the barn.

"I noticed there's a large section of the field that used to grow wheat," SP29 said.

"We don't have the manpower to do that now."

"You didn't, until now," SP29 corrected her. "I found your thresher in the barn. We can repair it, then clone seeds to start growing wheat."

The thought of eating bread again nearly made tears return to Hannah's eyes. It had been so *long* since she or any other New Edeners had enjoyed such a luxury. She willed the tears away. She'd spent more than enough time weeping lately, and it was getting embarrassing. "You could really do that?" she asked as she opened the barn door.

"I think the more immediate priority is saving what we can of the food already grown, but cultivating wheat is within our capabilities." A couple of cyborgs behind them joined in a chorus of yeses. "What do you think?"

"I agree," Hannah replied, hoping her voice didn't waver. "We've lost a lot of crops already, since there aren't enough hands to grow it." Baskets of tomatoes crammed every table in the canning area. God, she was sick of everything tomato-related, but the crops were stubborn, and there was enough to feed everyone. "Let me show you our canning equipment. The jars have been here since before I was born, and we don't have the means to produce new glass anymore, so you'll have to be careful with them. We have acidifiers made from the local sugar berries, so that'll make the process easier."

It didn't take long for the cyborgs to pick up the nuances of canning, New Eden-style. With their inhuman speed, she guessed that they could preserve a hundred kilos of food a day if they wanted to. As it was, within a few hours, every tomato they had picked that day was accounted for and ready for distribution, either in jars or fresh.

Hannah then showed the cyborgs their chicken coop. There were eight birds in all, including a pair of roosters, none of which could be eaten until their egg-laying days were behind them.

"I think you said you could clone them?" Hannah asked as she lifted a hen to check for eggs. It squawked in protest but didn't otherwise fight back.

"We can. We also collected the eggs earlier today."

"You've thought of everything, haven't you?"

SP29 gave a very human shrug. "This is too much for one person to do on her own."

"I'm not always alone. This is just the thing I keep working at more than anyone," Hannah explained. "I don't have much in the way of technical skills."

"We received your SOS," SP29 said, puzzled. "I would say your skills are adequate in that area."

"I found an old training manual that someone must've forgotten to throw away when they first colonized the planet. It was a lot of trial and error and some sheer dumb luck that I got the SOS out. It was rough." A small voice in the back of her mind asked her why she was saying this, putting down her skills and achievements when someone had just given her a compliment. She'd received so few of them, even before the quake. "Thank you," she said hurriedly. "It means a lot to know that someone with your level of experience with everything electric thinks I did okay."

"You saved both of our people. That's more than doing okay."

She felt herself blush at the compliment, but couldn't

resist saying, "It was a group effort. All of us have worked hard to keep ourselves alive."

"It was *your* SOS that brought us here. We wouldn't have bothered New Eden if not for your broadcast."

It was on the tip of her tongue to ask SP29 about their old home and the ion storm that destroyed it. She caught herself in time, not wanting to dredge up painful memories for him or the other cyborgs, and there was work to be done, besides. "It was a group effort on both sides," she replied. She looked around the barn. "Where did you put the eggs?"

———

FROM A STRICTLY TECHNICAL point of view, the power station wasn't in the dire straits Hannah assumed it was. As RH103 toured the facility with his fellow cyborgs, he thought they could probably have the entire facility up and running within the week.

"There's a lot of corrosion," he noted as he strode through the pump room. As Hannah had said, the station was powered by a waterfall only a kilometer away, one of dozens surrounding the planet's lone landmass and the largest. "The earthquake also knocked out a lot of the pipes that carried water into the facility."

"I'm surprised it hasn't flooded," said BE89 from behind him.

"I checked its foundations and safety enhancements. There are watertight bulkheads around the station to keep water out. The early New Eden settlers took precautions against flooding in the event of seismic activity. The barriers worked as they were supposed to, but we have a great deal of cleanup ahead."

"No one here is worried about a little hard work."

"I don't think physical exertion will be the issue," RH103 said. "We don't have the means to drain the bulkheads easily."

"Wouldn't there be pumps in place to drain the excess water?"

"The bulkheads weren't designed to hold water for two years, and a lot of the pumping equipment has corroded."

"Why not suction it out?" BE89 asked.

"Where would we put the water after?"

Color touched BE89's cheeks. "Good point."

RH103 suppressed a sigh at BE89's questions. His fellow cyborg wasn't stupid; he just didn't think things through in the way the rest of them did. RH103 wondered what the original BE89 had been, how he had influenced his clone. He hadn't been someone with scientific knowledge or a military background, that was obvious.

"The water could be repurposed. Maybe they'd like to have swimming pools in their yards," BE89 added.

Now it was everyone's turn to stare at BE89. It wasn't the first time he'd made an inane remark, but RH103 thought this was hardly appropriate. "What?"

BE89 held up his hands. "What? It was a joke."

Silence answered him.

"One day with humans and you're already making jokes?" The voice belonged to CW44. It was as rough and creaky as a malfunctioning door from disuse. He rarely spoke outside of their shared broadcast link.

BE89 shrugged. "Why not? We're among humans now. We should act like it."

The thought had crossed RH103's mind as well, particularly when it came to using a regular human name, and that he was living in a house. "This isn't the time for jokes. And we're already mostly human. We're just enhanced."

"We're enhanced copies of copies." BE89's eyes took

on a faraway look, as if he was lost in memory. "I don't want to be like that anymore."

The last thing RH103 wanted to do right now was reminisce over their originals.

"Perhaps this is a conversation to be had at another time."

BE89 sighed. "All right. But I'm not letting this go. It's going to take more than repairing New Eden's power station to fit in in this society."

"Don't you think we know that?" CW44 said flatly.

"Enough." RH103 faced all of them. "Whoever wants to discuss this later is welcome to. I promised Hannah Forsyth that I would have a plan and timelines for the station's repairs by tonight, and I intend to keep that promise."

Silence greeted him, and he wondered if he'd made a misstep. He'd never done that before.

"Why Hannah?" BE89 asked curiously.

"She's the settlement's unofficial leader, at least until they hold an election."

"Wouldn't Rodelle Lansing fit into that role?"

RH103 thought of the sad woman in the front row the previous night in the amphitheater and felt a twinge of sympathy. "Why would she?"

"She's the leader's widow," BE89 explained patiently. "Wouldn't she be entitled to that honor?"

"I don't think New Eden works that way. This isn't a monarchy. And how do you know who Mrs. Lansing is?"

"She's letting me live in her house. She's staying in her guesthouse at the back of the property."

The revelation sparked RH103's ire. "Why the hell are you in the house while she stays in her guesthouse?"

The other cyborg held up his hands in defense. "She

offered. She said she hasn't stayed there since her husband died. Says it has too many bad memories for her."

"I see. My apologies." But RH103 made a mental note to ask Mrs. Lansing about the arrangement. Ensure it truly worked for her. Despite his tendency to think and reason differently than the rest of them, BE89 was still thoughtful in a more human way than RH103 or the others were.

"I've also decided that I'm not going to be BE89 anymore," the cyborg continued. "Call me Brandon instead."

Everyone else stared at him, aghast.

RH103 searched his memory banks for the scant information he had on BE89's original. "Wasn't the first BE named Brayden Emerson?"

"Yes, but I don't like the name Brayden." BE89—Brandon—drew himself up to his full height, a determined look on his face. "And I'm not technically Brayden, just the eighty-ninth version of him. I like Brandon better. I'm just Brandon Emerson from now on."

If acknowledging BE89 as Brandon Emerson would make the power station repairs go that much faster, RH103 would do so. "Very well. Anyone else who wants to go by a different designation is free to do so, just tell us what to call you." He looked at the damaged pumps still waiting to be fixed. "Let's get that plan in place, like I promised."

CHAPTER FIVE

THE HOUSE WAS empty when Hannah returned in the evening, a wooden box of eggs in one hand and a basket of tomatoes and potatoes in the other. Her muscles ached from exertion, a familiar feeling, but it wasn't so uncomfortable tonight. She could have wept with how much had been accomplished that day, and the promise of more to come.

As she started preparing dinner, it felt as if a great weight had been lifted off her shoulders. Like her other neighbors after the quake, she had set up a firepit in her backyard to cook food over. She built up the flames, then set up a dented pot on a homemade stand over it, filled with water, to boil some eggs.

Jasmine walked out of her back door as Hannah sat back to keep an eye on the fire. She waved as she set up her own fire and a pot of something over the flames. As soon as the tinder was ablaze, she quickly crossed over to Hannah's yard.

"This is the most relaxed I've seen you look in years," Jasmine said by way of greeting.

"This *is* the most relaxed I've been in years. You should see the barn and the fields. Agricultural production has almost caught up since the cyborgs got here. Your new housemate just dove right in and started working."

"Without consulting you first?"

"I was surprised, but pleasantly so." Hannah leaned back, crossing her feet at the ankles. "It was a relief not to be in charge for a few hours, you know?"

Jasmine nodded. "I get the feeling, although we haven't had any cyborgs volunteer with textiles." Jasmine was a seamstress by trade but had a knack for repurposing almost anything. On a planet with almost nothing, its existing stock of housewares rapidly depleting due to age, it was a valuable skill.

"Would having some of them work with clothes or anything help? I can ask RH103 about that, although I'm not sure any of them would have experience with either."

"Clothes and making soap from tree sap is hardly a priority yet." Jasmine peeked over her shoulder, as if she expected one of the cyborgs to listen in on their conversation. Hannah already knew her next words would have nothing to do with textiles. "Are they hatched from tanks or something? I thought it might be rude to ask SP29."

"He's the friendliest cyborg I've met so far," Hannah replied. "I don't think he'd be offended if you asked how they reproduce. They're probably really proud of their cloning techniques. He's ready to start cloning cattle and chickens the first chance they get."

"Really?" Jasmine's face was hopeful. "I miss meat."

"Wheat too."

Her friend's face mirrored Hannah's feelings earlier in the day, when she thought about the possibility of eating bread again. "Oh, my God."

"I know."

Jasmine's voice dropped to a whisper. "Do you think they know about human methods of reproduction?"

Hannah felt herself blush. "I'm sure that's included in their data banks. Or brains, I don't know. I feel like they would have an instinct for what to do."

"Do you think they'd be interested in, well . . ." Jasmine shot a furtive look around their backyards, as if nervous that a cyborg might pop up out of nowhere. "Us?"

The image of RH103 in all of his flight-suited glory, hinting at an impressive physique, flashed in Hannah's mind. "Um," she said uselessly.

It was one thing to have a new roommate. It was another to have one she fantasized about. She didn't want to fall into that trap.

"I'm just saying, SP29 and that DL-whatever number guy are the finest examples of his species that I've seen," Jasmine said.

"I think they're technically the same species as us, just with a lot more wires. And I don't know which one DL is."

"The tanned one with short dark hair. And I haven't seen someone that hot, ever. Don't look at me like that," she sniffed.

"Like what?"

"Like I'm wrong. There was a distinct lack of eligible men before the earthquake, and there are none now."

Hannah hadn't thought about her dating life, or lack thereof, in years, but she knew Jasmine was right about the dearth of potential partners. The only brief relationship she'd ever had was with James Thierry when they were sixteen, a decade prior. James had disappeared five years ago, when he took a trip to the northern part of New Eden's landmass and never returned. It had been ill-advised and stupid. Everyone knew that the north was an inhospitable and uninhabitable wasteland.

She chose her next words carefully. "You're living together for the time being. Maybe it would be best to put a possible relationship with a cyborg on the back burner until he has his own house."

She made a face. "Ugh, I hate it when you're reasonable."

"Someone has to be."

"You've been reasonable for too long. You'll have an opportunity to relax soon. All of us will. Maybe you'll stop going to the fields to pick carrots in the middle of the night now."

Hannah rose to her feet to check on the eggs. They tumbled around merrily in the pot. Idly, she wondered if RH103 liked hard-boiled eggs. "You knew about that?"

"Of course I did. Everyone does. Weren't you doing that last night, when the cyborgs arrived?"

For some strange reason, she felt embarrassed to be called out about her late-night habits, her insomnia. "It needs to be done."

"You're already doing more than enough without sacrificing your sleep," Jasmine said.

"My being up worked out for all of us," Hannah pointed out. "You wouldn't have a hot cyborg in your house if I'd been sleeping."

"Sure, I would've. They're nice to us. They would have woken us up when they landed."

"Jasmine?"

SP29 waved from Jasmine's back porch, a basket of something in one gloved hand. His short dark hair was tousled, and his green eyes had an odd mirror effect, like RH103's did at certain angles. "Hi!" Jasmine said brightly. She got up and murmured, "One of my hot cyborgs calls. We'll have to talk about this another time."

As she returned to her yard, a bit of the tension

Hannah had been holding on to for years unknotted itself. When was the last time she and Jasmine had had a conversation that hadn't revolved around loss?

Jasmine laughed at something SP29 said before taking his basket and dropping potatoes into the pot she set up over the fire. Aside from SP29 being a cyborg, it was such a *normal* thing to witness—her friend being happy and flirty. SP29 wasn't hard on the eyes, either. Hannah could see why Jasmine was drawn to him.

She peered into the pot again and tried to guess how long the eggs had been in there. At least ten minutes, she reasoned. She'd forgotten to bring a timer with her, a testament to her exhaustion. She carefully removed the pot from its tripod and started back for the house.

Before she could make it to the door, she smacked into something solid and black-clad. Boiling water splashed her hand, drawing a yelp from her and sending the pot crashing to the grass. "Fuck!" she yelped and looked up to RH103's perpetually neutral expression.

Except, this time, concern flashed across his eyes when she saw her nursing her burned hand. "Let me see," he said, holding out his own gloved ones.

"It's fine," Hannah replied. She bent down to retrieve the eggs, noting that only a couple had cracked in their fall. "I didn't expect you to sneak up on me like that."

"My apologies. It wasn't deliberate."

"I know, and I'll be fine," she repeated.

"At least let me take the pot as an apology."

"You drive a hard bargain." Her hand really did smart against the burn. She handed the pot over to him and led him back into the house.

He had already used one of his battery cubes to charge the kitchen lights. Their glow hadn't been seen since before the earthquake, and Hannah blinked in surprise at the welcome sight. "Wow," she said in appreciation, her burn temporarily forgotten.

"I know it's a little early for light, but I thought you'd appreciate it."

"I do," she said, touching the wall lamp with her good hand.

"You'll need some water on that burn," RH103 reminded her. He put the plug in the sink and worked the kitchen pump until cold water flowed from it, filling the basin.

It wasn't that bad. It would leave a red mark that would fade in a day or two. But it had been so long since Hannah had anyone to care about her in this way that she obediently stuck her hand into the sink. "I hope you like hard-boiled eggs," she said.

"My original liked poached eggs. I'm sure their hard-boiled counterparts will be fine."

The mention of RH103's original piqued her curiosity. Before she could talk herself out of it, she asked, "Do you know a lot about your original? I guess that's the person you were cloned from?"

He was quiet for a few seconds, and she wondered if she'd overstepped.

"I have some of his memories," RH103 replied. "I know his name. Actually, I was thinking of using it instead of my numerical designation."

"Oh?"

"The subject of names came up earlier today at the power station," he continued. "BE89 has announced that he is to be called Brandon going forward. I think using regular names is a good way to fit in, so I have decided to go by Rhys."

He delivered the news with a waver in his voice, so different from his usual near-flat effect, as if he was worried about how Hannah would receive it.

Nonsense. Calling him by a regular name would definitely be easier. "Rhys," she said aloud. "I guess that's what the R stands for in your name?"

"The one hundredth and third clone of Rhys Hammond."

Hannah unplugged the sink and dried off her hand with a homemade towel embroidered by her mother, wrapping it in the worn fabric to soothe the burn. "I think it's wild that there were 102 of you before."

"We're all a little different. Most of the clones were hatched and terminated decades ago, as the technology was being perfected. I've been the only RH clone for twenty-eight years."

That made him close to the same age as her, at least physically. "How did the rest die?"

He hesitated. "Early clones often failed due to faults in their genetic manipulation or faulty cybernetics, sometimes both." His answer was rushed, as if there was more to the story, but he didn't want to talk about it. He pointed at the basket of tomatoes resting on the small counter next to the sink. "What do you wish to do with these?"

She took the hint. He didn't want to talk about his previous clones. "A salad, I guess. I have zucchini and corn too. No lettuce, though. Most of it died in the last crop because we couldn't harvest it quickly enough before the rainy season."

"I'll roast everything outside," Rhys promised.

Hannah looked at the kitchen's outside door. Through the empty space where a screen was once nailed, she could see that the fire still burned. "Damn it," she muttered.

"What is it?"

"I left the fire alone. I swear to God I'm not usually so

irresponsible." She leaned against the counter, holding her wrapped hand against her.

"You've hardly slept since we arrived," Rhys replied. "I was also looking out for the fire. It's contained." He put a hand on her shoulder, a clumsy gesture at comfort.

She could feel the heat of him through his gloves and her T-shirt's fabric. It was an innocent move, one that felt like he was imitating humans he'd seen in old holographs, rather than from a place of compassion, but she felt it as acutely as the burn making her hand throb. It shouldn't make her breath catch, but it did. She thought back to her earlier conversation with Jasmine, who'd been so excited at the possibility of having a cyborg clone boyfriend.

Stop that. Don't think of RH103—Rhys—as a potential boyfriend. That's probably the worst thing to be doing right now.

Both of them were trying to rebuild their lives, establish a new normal for their respective people. They needed clear heads for that. *Hannah* needed a clear head for that. She was sure Rhys wouldn't have such problems.

"Hannah?"

She blinked and Rhys removed his hand. Idly, she wondered what his looked like under the gloves. She'd only seen a brief glimpse when he'd unlocked his ship.

"I can finish making our meal," Rhys said. "That's within my capabilities."

"I can help," she said, turning around to remove a bottle of dried wild basil from the spice rack her father built decades ago, but Rhys took it from her.

"I can manage this," he promised. "I won't be long." He gathered some of the vegetables resting on the counter and tucked them into the tomato basket, along with the spices Hannah picked out. Without another word, he left the kitchen.

She stared at his retreating back, surprise holding her in place against the tile floor.

It was nice to have someone else cook for her.

She unwrapped her hand and flexed it, inspecting the damage. As she suspected, there wasn't any significant damage, but she still appreciated Rhys's concern. She hadn't had a warm and fuzzy feeling like that since long before the earthquake.

She set the table and rummaged around a cabinet for a bottle of dandelion wine from her modest stash. Indecision warred within her. Did cyborgs drink? Would it have any negative effects on his electronics?

She shrugged and set it on the table, then set to peeling the hard-boiled eggs.

Rhys returned a short time later, bearing roasted vegetables. He and Hannah took seats at the table across from each other, and she nudged the bowl of eggs to him. "Help yourself."

He speared two with his fork and set them on his plate. "Thank you."

"I should be thanking you," she corrected. "And I probably will every day for the rest of my life."

"I also mean, thank you for sharing a meal with me. For sharing your home."

She felt herself flush. "It's nice to have company."

"What about your friends? You were speaking with your neighbor earlier. You two seem close, at least to me." He hesitated for a second. "I'm unsure about regular human interaction."

The thought of Jasmine and how she'd pulled away from her oldest and dearest friend sent shame and guilt spiraling through Hannah. She hadn't deserved Jasmine's easy camaraderie or forgiveness. "We are," she said. "We've known each other our whole lives. Our parents were friends, our grandparents were friends, going all the way back to New Eden's colonization."

"I have a lot of questions about the early colonists."

"So do I, mostly about how shortsighted and ignorant they were. You can't hide from technology or the rest of the galaxy forever."

"Has the planet never had contact with another people since the settlement was built?"

Hannah shook her head. "The first colonists brought everything they needed to create a self-sustaining community with them. We knew other species and cultures exist but don't have a way of contacting anyone."

"The lack of interplanetary trade is alarming."

"Yeah, no shit. I'm sure there's any number of medical treatments we're missing out on." She tried not to let bitterness lace her words. She ate a few mouthfuls of food before speaking again. "What about you? Who decided Rhys Hammond needed to be cloned and cybernetically enhanced?" He'd seemed comfortable talking about Rhys, even if he wasn't about his other clones.

"I believe it was the original Rhys Hammond himself, but I'm not sure."

Hannah leaned back in her chair, wanting to hear more. "Oh?"

"A lot of our shared information from the early years of the cyborg and cloning project was deleted by our originals," he explained. "We haven't found a way to recover it yet. We've been taking care of ourselves and cloning each other as necessary for a long time. I don't remember a great deal before that time of my original or the clones before me. Just pieces here and there."

It was fucked up, but he didn't seem too upset about it. Curious, maybe. "Doesn't it upset you that all that information was erased? Who wanted to keep it a secret and why?"

A shadow crossed over Rhys's face, a very human expression. "That's something we've long wanted to discover. We thought it had to be for something nefarious. Tools of war, perhaps. But there weren't any major wars occurring anywhere in the galaxy at the time when I suspect the original Rhys was cloned. Only minor local conflicts that wouldn't have required the use of super soldiers that cyborgs can be programmed to be.

"We have no memory or records of organic leadership," he continued. "Someone organic had to enhance our originals and start the cloning process. Our theory is that our predecessors rebelled and killed whoever created them and restarted their lives aboard our ship. We're certain our predecessors didn't build it."

The nonchalant way he spoke of one of his former incarnations being a killer sent a chill zipping down Hannah's spine. Her hand hovered over her plate, and a piece of roasted tomato slipped off it. Who the hell had she just invited to live with her people?

Rhys picked up on her change in demeanor. "Hannah, are you worried about that?"

She thought about Jasmine hosting SP29 next door and already crushing on him and that other DL-whatever cyborg. Then her mind wandered over to how helpful everyone had been in the barn, to the plans Rhys presented to her regarding the power station's repairs. He'd even said he wanted to be more human while he was here, hence his name change.

Humans can kill other people too. They were sort of famous for it.

Rhys was still waiting for an answer. *Might as well be honest.* "A little bit, yeah." Her voice shook the way her hand did when she tried to re-spear the tomato chunk with her fork.

"*We* aren't like that," he said firmly. "If our predecessors killed anyone, they would have done so for serious reasons. We've discussed the possibility at length. We have avoided conflict and contact with others and kept to ourselves until now. Like you, we're a people of peace."

She relaxed a little. She believed him, faster than she probably should have.

She was so tired of being hopeless; everyone was. She'd known deep down that, if the cyborgs hadn't shown up when they did, New Eden would have died out sooner rather than later. Its infrastructure was too damaged, so much of the population had been lost and wasn't being replaced, and the lack of tech had turned into a death sentence. Hannah supposed New Eden still had nothing to lose by welcoming the cyborgs to live among them.

"I don't know if we're particularly peaceful. Once you've been here longer, you'll see how we bicker with each other." She looked at the unopened bottle of wine on the table. "Want a drink?"

He looked at it, hesitation and indecision warring on his face, before nodding. Hannah uncorked the bottle and poured glasses for each of them. He picked up his and sniffed it, features contorted.

"It's wine, or New Eden's version of it. Dandelions are good for something," Hannah said.

"I know. I've smelled it before, but I can't place it."

"Maybe the original Rhys liked it."

He took another cautious sniff. "Possibly."

Hannah raised her glass. "To fixing New Eden and giving you a new home."

Rhys looked at her raised glass, puzzled, before copying

her movement. Hannah clinked her glass against his before taking a sip.

He did likewise, made the same face as before, and set it down. "That was a toast," she added.

"You do this before drinking?"

"Only if it's a special occasion. Old Earther custom." She thought about her parents, who found an excuse to toast whenever they opened a bottle. "Or if you just feel like it. I haven't had the chance to do that with anyone since . . ." She didn't want to bring up the quake again. "In a long time," she quickly finished.

"To new beginnings, then," Rhys said, raising his glass again. Hannah smiled and tapped hers against it.

Her gaze caught his across the table. There was a strange intensity reflected in his dark eyes that made her breath catch, and she was unable to look away. For a second, she remembered Jasmine's quips about having a hot new roommate.

Just as quickly, the moment was gone, but her friend's suggestions still echoed in her mind. She dearly hoped cyborgs couldn't read regular human minds too.

"To new beginnings," she repeated, and took another fortifying sip of wine.

CHAPTER SIX

An unfamiliar metallic taste filled Rhys's mouth as he stared into the seemingly bottomless pool of black water that filled the flooded bulkhead. His heart skipped a couple of beats. His cybernetics told him that there was nothing wrong with his pulmonary functions. Instead, the cause of his heart's irregularities was the rarest reason of them all: unknown physiological causes.

It took another few seconds for Rhys to realize what he was experiencing—fear.

He was afraid of deep water.

He closed his eyes and locked down his connection to the cyborgs' broadcast link, not wanting his brethren to know how he felt. It was completely irrational. He was a *cyborg*. He had underwater breathing capabilities. He didn't know why he had them, since he had never had the opportunity to go deep sea diving while living aboard a space-faring vessel, but there must have been a reason his original cyborg unit was designed with such capabilities. Perhaps the original Rhys Hammond was afraid of water and this was simply a residual feeling.

He tore his vision away from the flooded bulkhead and steeled himself. Closing his eyes, he focused on the pleasant heat New Eden's twin suns left on his exposed skin. He breathed deeply, noting the scents of earth and grass surrounding the power station.

He was being ridiculous. His programming meant he knew how to swim. The bulkhead was eight meters deep, hardly life-threatening to a being like him.

Rhys opened his eyes to see the other cyborgs on the edges of their respective bulkheads, standing on the flimsy platforms in little more than their flight trousers. Metal components embedded in their skin flashed in the sunlight as a further reminder that they were impervious to drowning.

Let's get this over with.

All they had to do was get into the bulkheads and open the drains, diverting the trapped water into the nearby river. It was easy enough and shouldn't take longer than ten minutes if he concentrated. BE89—Brandon, he reminded himself again—had already spent plenty of time in the water, both in the drains and in the river, to make sure the pipes were still functioning. He'd come out none the worse for wear.

I'm a leader, damn it. I should be able to do this.

Splashes around him alerted him to his fellow cyborgs already jumping in. He was the last cyborg standing on his bulkhead's platform.

He took a deep breath and jumped in feet first.

Panic clawed at him as the shock of cold water overloaded his senses. He forced his eyes open and activated his night vision function, so he could better see the drains lining the bulkhead as he slowly sank to the bottom. Water filled his nose and throat, making him cough and choke.

I'm malfunctioning!

He tried to call for help, but nothing came out. He thought about Hannah, how he had failed her and her people.

She would be working in a field right now, probably chatting with SP29. When he thought about them talking and laughing, jealousy clawed at him, warring with his panic.

RH103? Are you all right?

Brandon's voice filled his head, and Rhys realized his broadcast link had reactivated itself. Great, now everyone was feeling him drown.

No, Rhys replied. He hated to admit that but didn't want to lie.

You can breathe in there, I promise. The other cyborg's voice was calm and rational, almost soothing. *It's all right to be afraid of this. We've never seen this much water in one place. Breathe in through your nose.*

Rhys tried but coughed again.

You're fighting it, Brandon continued. *You're not going to drown. If you were, you would have already. Don't think about the water. Pretend you're on land.*

As if he could pretend the weight of hundreds of liters of water wasn't pressing around him. Rhys took a shallow breath, hating the sensation of fluid in his nasal passages and throat, but he didn't sputter again. Some of his panic ebbed away, and he was able to focus on the nearest drain lock. He twisted it open.

I've opened a drain, he reported back to Brandon.

One down, four to go. The other cyborg's voice was annoyingly chipper. He sounded more organic than machine in that moment. Not for the first time, he wondered what Brandon's original had been.

Only four more drains to unlock, then the worst part of the power station's restoration would be over. He pictured Hannah, how happy she would be when it was restored. He wanted to see her smile again, smile at *him*.

He was doing this for Hannah.

The thought of her bolstered him as he crept along the bulkhead's sides, unlocking drains. The sound of water rushing through them filled his ears and kept trying to pull him back under until his hands found the metal ladder hugging the wall. A measure of relief filled him as he gripped the supports and hauled himself up.

Brandon was standing on the bulkhead platform when he emerged from the water. He involuntarily gasped for air as he did so, then splayed himself on the platform under the sun.

An old memory of a starfish on a pink sand beach flashed into his mind, undoubtedly one of the original Rhys's. He'd never been on a beach in his existence.

"RH103," Brandon said, crouching down. "Are you all right?"

Rhys nodded, eyes closed against the sun's glare. "Apologies," he said. He coughed again, metallic-tasting water dribbling from his mouth. "I did not know until now that I don't care for deep water."

Brandon gave a very human shrug. It was remarkable how quickly he had adapted to living with organics, compared to the rest of them. "Hopefully, we'll only have to do this once. The water's draining as it should, and the bulkheads should be empty within the next couple of hours." He stood up and held out his hand.

Rhys stared at it, then at Brandon's face.

"I'm offering to help you up," Brandon said.

"Why?"

"You've never been laid out on a bulkhead after thinking you're about to drown. It seemed the kind thing to do."

Rhys let Brandon help him to his feet. He swayed a little and coughed, sputtering water. "Thank you."

"You're welcome." Brandon's eyes searched Rhys's face, as if he was looking for further confirmation that he was truly all right. "Maybe you should sit down for a while, get your bearings back."

"My functions are optimal now that I'm out of the water. I'll dry off and get back to work." Already, Rhys could feel his body's reactions returning to normal. His panic and the resulting spike in adrenaline receded.

He wanted to have good news for Hannah at the end of the day. Since he'd met her, all he wanted to see was a measure of relief on her face, a smile directed at him.

He could tell Brandon didn't believe him, but the other cyborg didn't argue. "If you say so, RH103."

Rhys shook his head. "Just call me Rhys."

Brandon's eyebrow raised in surprise.

"Everyone who has taken on a normal human name has been correct in doing so," Rhys explained. "We're living among organics now."

"You do realize that we're mostly organic, don't you?"

But it wasn't the same. It wasn't just about their physical bodies and enhancements. Rhys was at a loss when it came to the corresponding emotions and expressions. He wasn't picking them up as easily as everyone else seemed to be. "Yes," he replied evenly.

"Is that your original's name?"

Rhys nodded.

"Have you considered taking something else? You aren't him and don't have to be."

Rhys shook his head. "Rhys is as good a name as any. I've inherited his fondness for eggs and fear of deep water. I don't see why I should change it." Finding another name would take too much time, besides.

"Solid reasoning." Brandon looked at the bulkhead, its water level rapidly receding. "Go dry off and I'll meet you inside."

———

BY THE TIME the twin suns set, Rhys and the other cyborgs had a plan and timeline for resurrecting the power station. Some of the hydraulic components needed to be replaced after rusting through, but that would be easily accomplished using their ship's hard goods replicator.

When he thought about Hannah on his walk home, his heart did the same inexplicable flip-flopping as it had earlier. He wanted to hear about her day, tell her about the progress being made on the power station. To see her smile in relief, see those lines of tension and exhaustion smooth away from her face. He wondered what she looked like when she was happy.

I wonder what I would look like if I was happy? He'd never experienced that before. Contentment, certainly. He wasn't sure he could experience happiness the way organics or some of his other cyborgs did.

He found her in the backyard, watching a pot of something boiling over the firepit. She sat on the grass, arms loosely wrapped around her bent knees. A smile bloomed on her face when she saw him, and with it, a sense of relief trickled through him. He joined her, grateful to finally be sitting down. "How was your day?" he asked by way of greeting.

"Pretty good. We're getting ready to plant your fancy enhanced wheat seeds," she replied. "SP29 thinks we could have a crop ready to harvest in less than a month." She turned shining eyes to him. "I can't tell you how excited I am to eat bread again. I had no idea you could grow wheat so quickly."

Jealousy flashed in him at the mention of SP29 and how his wheat seeds brought her such joy. It was quickly followed by irritation at himself for feeling that way when SP29's actions would benefit everyone. "How long does wheat usually take here?"

"About four months. Our crops were grown from the traditional seeds our ancestors brought to New Eden."

He nearly pointed out how inefficient that was, but didn't bother. Hannah already knew that and decried how the first settlers stubbornly clung to traditional ways. "I have good news too. The power station should be fully functional within the next 48 hours."

His words had the intended effect. "Oh, my God!" Before he could react, she threw her arms around him in a fierce hug, squeezing him with all her might. It took a couple of seconds for his brain to recognize what was happening. She pulled away before his programming fully recognized the gesture as affectionate. Instantly, he regretted that he'd missed his chance to reciprocate. "Sorry," she breathed. "That's incredible news. I guess today went well for you, then?"

He considered telling her of his newly discovered fear of water, but didn't. It was embarrassing and probably a fluke. He'd never experienced it before and would be fine the next time he had to jump into a flooded bulkhead.

The memory of thousands of liters of dank-smelling water pressing on his body, entering his nose, slammed into him. He willed it away. "It did. Once we drained the bulkheads, everything else fell into place."

"It went swimmingly." She laughed at her words.

"I'm sorry?"

"It's a stupid joke, is all. Lots of water, you had to get in —it went swimmingly."

"How do you know I was the one in the water?"

"I can smell it on you. You smell like the falls."

Rhys wasn't sure how to feel about that. He thought about the smell and taste of it and fought back a shudder. "Is that bad?"

"No. When I'm not facing certain death due to starvation and natural disasters, I like going there. It's very pretty." She stood up and peered into the pot. She unhooked it from its tripod. "I'll have to take you there someday. Maybe you'll like it."

He rose too. "I'm certain I will." As long as he didn't have to go over one of them.

She changed the subject. "Are you okay with eggs again?"

"Yes."

"We'll have proper meat soon enough, but this will have to do for now. Jasmine brought over some bean and cucumber salad today too."

"Whatever we have on hand is sufficient."

"You're so easy to please."

Perhaps it was the teasing tone of voice she used that made a frisson of awareness zing through him at that statement. "What pleases you?" he returned.

She paused at the back door to stare at him for a moment. Color bloomed in her cheeks. "I . . ." She cleared her throat. "I don't know anymore."

"Power?" he tried.

Her eyes widened in response, and he wondered if he'd made a misstep. Another one, judging by her physical reaction to his question. "Yes," she said slowly.

"What else?"

She opened the door and held it for him. "I'm not sure if I'm ready for this conversation," she muttered.

"Why not?"

"You're really innocent in a lot of ways, aren't you?"

"I don't understand. Have I upset you?" He set the pot in the kitchen sink and pumped cold water over it to cool down the eggs.

"No." She nudged him out of the way to take over the dinner prep. "You can go ahead and sit down. I'll take care of this."

He waited until both of them sat down at the table to ask, "How am I innocent?"

"Maybe 'innocent' isn't the best word. 'Inexperienced' might be better."

"I'm inexperienced in a lot of things," Rhys replied. "That doesn't mean I can't learn."

She regarded him thoughtfully for a moment. For the first time, he fiercely wished that he could read her mind like he could with the other cyborgs. Or for his sensors to detect more about her than her core body temperature, which was normal for a human. "I'm sure you could," she said. "I bet you're a quick study."

He'd heard that term before, but not as the 103rd iteration of Rhys Hammond. His fork hovered over his plate as he tried to remember.

A giant of a man in a dark gray uniform, similar to the matching flight suits all of the current cyborgs wore, yelled at him about not being fast enough at something. Was it exterior repairs in zero-g? Had he erred in repairs and was now facing consequences for it? "I thought you were a quick study," the man in gray shouted at him. "A quick fucking study! And then this happens!" He reached for a small pen-shaped device at his belt and jammed it into Rhys's neck. Then everything went black.

"Rhys?"

Hannah's voice snapped him out of the memory. He dropped his fork with a clatter against the plate. "You just blanked out for a minute there," she said. "Are you okay?"

This was the second time today that something had him frozen in place, although he wasn't sure what he had just remembered. He had the distinct feeling that he had just watched and felt one of his previous clones be killed. "Yes," he lied.

The look she gave him told him plainly that she didn't believe him, but she didn't push. He appreciated that. He had no idea how to feel about resurfacing memories of people who technically weren't him. He wondered if the other cyborgs were experiencing something similar and if he should bring it up on their shared broadcast the next time they were in range of each other. But surely, if one of the others was having memories of his original and iterations, he would have said something.

After dinner, Hannah announced that she would visit with her friend next door and left the house after cleaning the dishes. He took a cold bath in the tub upstairs, wanting to get the smell of the bulkhead water off him.

According to his sensors, the bathwater was a bare fourteen degrees. While he could tolerate the cold, he hated to think that the unenhanced Hannah had been enduring this for years. "Hot water," he murmured aloud. "She's going to be so happy with hot water."

He helped himself to her soap, a handmade waxy square that smelled of mint and something flowery. His cybernetics identified it as being sap-based, probably from the trees native to New Eden, and the same substance used for the planet's candle supply. The soap was only one of the scents he noticed on her skin. The other was that of the sun, a smell he hadn't known existed until he met her.

What was she doing at her friend's house? Curiosity pulled at him at what she and Jasmine could be talking about. Perhaps his lack of social graces in relation to the rest of the cyborgs? SP29, Brandon, and everyone else seemed to be having an easier time adapting to organic living.

Her comment about him being inexperienced wounded his pride. How the hell was he supposed to gain experience, and in what areas did he need it?

The bathwater's chill suddenly reached him. His teeth chattered for the first time. Perhaps this was the organic experience he needed, he thought as he stepped out of the tub. Wrapping a towel around himself, he hoped he could hone in on the other areas where he needed it.

———

JASMINE WAS ONLY TOO happy to see Hannah on her doorstep. "Come in!" she said excitedly. "SP29's down at the barn, trying to grow a chicken in a tube or something, I didn't quite get it when he explained it to me. We'll have *meat* again soon! Do you want some wine? I have a couple of bottles I've been saving."

"Keep on saving them. I had some last night."

Jasmine looked at her quizzically. "You don't drink alone." She held open the door and Hannah walked through.

"I wasn't. Rhys had some too."

"Is that what RH103 is calling himself now?"

"Yeah, he said it's his original's name. I guess SP29 hasn't jumped on board that train?"

"He hasn't mentioned anything about that to me yet. Is dandelion tea all right? I just boiled some water."

"Thank you." Hannah followed Jasmine through the

foyer to the kitchen. Her friend's house was smaller than Hannah's, not meant to house more than one or two people. It was one floor, with a combined living room and kitchen off the foyer. Two small bedrooms and a bathroom were on the other side of the house, one of the bedrooms barely large enough to hold a bed. Jasmine used it as a lab of sorts, for creating the planet's supply of soap and candles. The house was filled with the pleasant scent of tree sap.

"How is it living with SP29?" Hannah asked while Jasmine fixed the tea.

"Cramped, but since we get along well, I don't mind it too much." They took seats on her couch, its cushion covers made from repurposed garments. A couple of blankets were folded on one of the arms. This was probably where SP29 slept. "What about Rhys?"

"He's a bit weird." Hannah may as well get that out now.

"Well, yeah, they're all a bit weird. So are we. We have to be the only planet in existence that has never had contact with other people until now." Jasmine looked up in excitement over her teacup's rim. "SP29 wants to make an off-world supply run sometime, and he said I could go with him."

"They're leaving?" Hannah couldn't keep the dismay out of her voice. The idea of Rhys taking off didn't sit right with her, as odd as he was.

"Not leaving, like they'll never return, but he said at some point, we're going to need supplies we can't create here. Building materials, medicine. You know that. I think the days of New Eden being the center of its own universe are numbered." She blew away some steam before taking a sip. "I welcome change."

So did Hannah. It was the whole reason she had

cobbled together a communications system to broadcast a distress call. "You're right."

Jasmine lifted an eyebrow. "Is there something you want to tell me?"

"I can't just visit for the hell of it?"

"You haven't since the quake. And I'm not upset about that," Jasmine quickly added. "You lost a lot in it and everyone grieves differently. I knew you'd come around when you were ready."

Hannah had gone to Jasmine's with the vague notion of talking about Rhys with her. The reminder of her lack of visits made her feel like a shitty friend. "I'm sorry," she said quietly.

"Don't be. I know what it's like. Maybe not the way you do, since I had a chance to say goodbye, but I know grief."

Jasmine's parents had died ten years apart, her mother most recently, about six months before the quake. Hannah had spent many nights at her house, knowing she didn't want to be alone. "Yeah," Hannah replied. "I didn't see the point of unloading on you when everyone else has experienced loss. None of us who survived didn't lose someone close to us."

"I didn't. You survived."

"I miss them." Hannah had never moved out of her parents' house on her own, preferring to stay put, instead of fixing up one of the empty houses that littered the settlement. Or had, until the quake destroyed most of them and rendered others unsafe to live in. They'd been close, her favorite people in the small world that was New Eden. The threat of tears loomed behind her eyes, but she willed them away and reminded herself why she was here. "I'm not here to talk about my parents or the earthquake."

"Yeah, tell me more about Rhys. Is he a good weird or a bad weird?"

Hannah quickly revised her earlier thoughts about favorite people. Her parents and Jasmine were equals in that category. "Definitely not a bad weird. I think he's just not used to living with humans, and he's having some difficulty adjusting. It's like night and day when I talk to him, compared to when I talk with SP29."

Jasmine nodded. "Aside from the power nodes in his hands and his eyes, you'd never know he was a cyborg."

"What power nodes?" It occurred to Hannah that she'd never seen Rhys without his gloves.

"It's so they can connect physically to their spaceship or something like that. SP29 said they can be used as weapons, too, which I guess could be helpful. He can burn through a tree in about ten seconds. It's amazing."

"Why would he need to burn down a tree?"

"Probably to impress me. It worked. And it was a rag bush, so technically not a tree."

Rag bushes were native to New Eden and interfered with their crops, so Hannah was happy to see them destroyed. Her curiosity was piqued. "How did he do it? And what would we have done if he'd started a fire?"

"He touched the bush's trunk, concentrated, and then burned through it. There wasn't a fire, just the smell of burning." She set her teacup on the coffee table. Hannah noticed she didn't elaborate on what she would have done in the case of fire. "Tell me about Rhys. You keep distracting me."

Hannah carefully chose her words. "I think he wants to talk, but he doesn't know how." Catching Jasmine's bemused look, she added, "I know you know what that's like. Rhys gets these . . . flashbacks, I guess. He says he's getting old memories from his original. Has that happened with SP29?"

Jasmine shook her head. "He's never said anything. Mostly, we just flirt."

"How the hell is he learning how to do that?"

"Beats me. Maybe it's reflexes from his original, I don't know. But I'm not going to not talk to someone who thinks I have beautiful eyes or likes my decorating. It's been a long time since anyone's paid me compliments."

When Hannah thought about flirting and compliments, she thought about Rhys's question about what pleased her. The man had a deep, quietly authoritative voice that had done things to her insides when he'd asked that. It was a little unsettling, and she couldn't tell if that was a good or bad thing.

"Rhys doesn't do that," she said. She paused, choosing her words carefully. "He's happy to tell me how things are progressing, even though he isn't exactly waving around pom-poms while he does it, you know?" That reminded her of something important. "Oh, we're probably going to have the power switched on in the next day or two."

"What the hell? Why couldn't you have begun with that?" Jasmine exclaimed in mock protest.

"Because I came here to talk about Rhys."

"Yeah, because you like him. It's okay if you do. I'd climb SP29 like a tree if he wanted me to. DL16 too." Her eyes glazed over. "Or both."

"My God. Do either of them want you to?"

"I think so, but SP29 has also talked about moving out with some cyborg friends once a suitable house is built. If he's going to make a move, he'll probably do it then. It'll make things less complicated than if we were still living together." She picked up her tea and took a healthy swallow. "At least, I hope he does. It's entirely possible I'm making up the vibes I think I'm feeling from him out of desperation and loneliness." She poked Hannah's leg with her foot. "Stop deflecting."

"*You* said you wanted to bang SP29 and DL16."

"Stop being logical and tell me about Rhys and why you like him."

There was no point in denying it. "I think I do," Hannah said quietly. "I don't know why, because it's not like we have a lot in common."

"You're both the de facto leaders of your respective societies that are facing extinction."

"I'm hardly a leader. And I'm sure there's some decorum to be expected if there is."

"You're the closest thing we have to that. You sent out that SOS. You've been working night and day since the quake to keep us fed. You convinced everyone that letting the cyborgs live here was a good idea and arranged billeting for them. You stepped up in a way no one else did."

"You looked after reusing old materials and repurposing things . . ." Hannah began, but Jasmine cut her off.

"Which is important, but you kept the planet fed. That was a huge responsibility, and it isn't only yours now." Jasmine rearranged herself, so her back was to the couch's arm. "Your tea's getting cold."

Hannah picked up her cup and drank some. "He understands responsibility," she said. "He's always so eager to tell me what he's accomplished during the day. He doesn't smile when he does it, but . . ."

"You can tell," Jasmine surmised.

"Yeah. But it's not like I smile that much, either."

Jasmine shrugged. "You'd be a perfect match."

"We hardly know each other," Hannah protested. "And

how do I know if I feel this way only because he's the first attractive man I've come across since the earthquake?"

"Since before the earthquake. I think a lot of the women here were ready to build their own spaceship and take off for parts unknown to find a partner they liked. I definitely was."

Hannah had to admit that Jasmine was right. Due to an aging, shrinking population, there'd been a distinct lack of spouses available in recent years. Even her brief relationship with James Thierry so many years ago was borne out of curiosity, not true affection or attraction. While the first settlers had large families, the last couple of generations had seen people having only one or two children, if that. The lack of medical care and poorly maintained infrastructure only added to their population woes.

"What do I do?" Hannah finally asked.

"Follow your instincts."

"They haven't been helpful."

"They're out of practice. They'll come back. In the meantime, just treat Rhys normally, like the leader of his people that he is. He respects you."

Beneath her conflicting feelings for the puzzling cyborg who shared her home, Hannah respected Rhys too. "I don't want to make things weird," she said.

"You won't. Just keep doing what you're doing and see how you feel in a while. Maybe Rhys will open up to you himself."

"Maybe." She drank some more tea, savoring its pleasant roasted taste. "Thank you."

CHAPTER SEVEN

THE POWER STATION'S control room was smaller than Rhys would have expected it to be, only large enough to hold perhaps four people. A wall of old-fashioned switches and levers faced him, all ready to be activated.

They'd done it. New Eden was about to have electricity for the first time in over two years. It had taken a couple of days past his original estimate of 48 hours to finish the repairs, thanks to a blocked bulkhead, but the people of New Eden hadn't cared. Hannah had organized a meeting in the amphitheater the night before to announce the impending repair, news that was met with resounding cheers.

And Hannah had looked at him with shining eyes and a smile that tugged at him. He'd even summoned a smile of his own in response. He wanted to see her look at him like that again.

Which was why she was with him now in the power station's control room. He thought she should have the honor of reactivating the power grid. She looked at the array of controls, a furrow between her brows. "You've made a lot of changes since I sent out that SOS," she said.

"Of course. We've made a number of improvements and reinforcements to protect the station, in the event of more seismic activity. That's why reactivating the power took so long. It will withstand another earthquake. We will also train your people to operate this equipment."

"I guess anything is an improvement from the old equipment." She peered at a row of newly installed controls. "You've restored the power in less than a week. That's hardly a long time."

"We had to build and replicate some components. Eventually, we will have to leave New Eden in search of raw materials that aren't available here. There's a waystation in this quadrant that's likely to have the supplies. There are more improvements still to be made."

"This is a hell of a start."

Rhys nodded at the controls. "You should switch it on."

She looked at him, aghast. "How?"

Rhys quickly activated the controls that would bring the power grid online. Gears shifted and whined. Engines whirred. A faint vibration reverberated through his boots. The last one was a lever that would bring electricity back to New Eden. "Pull down."

Hannah wrapped her hand around it and did so. A groan sounded from the wall before ceiling-mounted lights flickered to life, flooding the room with illumination. It dwarfed the light offered by battery cube-powered lanterns.

"Oh, my God!" Hannah bolted from the room to the corridor, where the lights blazed. "You really did it!"

"It was a group effort," Rhys replied. He would have said more, except she threw her arms around him like she had the other night in her backyard. His heart and breath stuttered at the contact, but at least this time, he had the wherewithal to return her embrace.

The top of her head barely reached his chin. Wisps of curly brown hair that had escaped its braid tickled his skin, a curious sensation. But that was nothing compared to the feel of her against him, her arms twined around his neck. He hadn't had that kind of contact with someone before. He hadn't known until now that he wanted it. She felt good in his arms, like she belonged there.

She pressed a kiss to his cheek. "Thank you," she whispered.

His whole body went on high alert, and he thought his programming might have gone offline for a moment. A strange heat raced through him, but his sensors said his core temperature was still normal. His heart rate increased again as it tended to do when he was around her, but he was starting to recognize that as a symptom induced by her presence. Nothing to worry about.

He returned the gesture, pressing his lips to her cheek in an imitation of hers. "You're welcome."

She looked at him in surprise, an unreadable expression on her face. Not that he was very good at reading human emotions. But she didn't run away or rebuke him, or even pull away. Her pupils flared against her hazel irises, and her breath came a little faster, signs Rhys recognized as arousal. Why he knew that, he couldn't say.

Perhaps that explained the thrum of unfamiliar energy and urges flooding him.

Neither of them spoke. Rhys was afraid to, not wanting to ruin the moment. His gloved hands remained firmly planted against her waist, holding her to him.

Hannah moved first. She closed her eyes and tilted her face toward him. An instinct Rhys didn't know he had until now had him lowering his head until his lips brushed hers with the barest of movements.

His body's processes and sensors lit up like the power grid just did. But before he could lean into her, taste her again, Brandon called out from the corridor. "Rhys?"

Hannah pulled away, putting a meter between them before Brandon stuck his head in the doorway. "The coupler that joins the westernmost part of the grid overheated," the other cyborg announced, a little too cheerfully for Rhys's liking. "The power failed in that part."

It took a few seconds for Rhys to find his voice and resist the impulse to throttle Brandon for the interruption. "We knew that was a possibility, since it's the oldest part of the grid."

"The western part was connected to the old spaceport," Hannah replied. Her voice sounded rougher than usual. "It won't impact residential homes or the agri center."

"We need the spaceport back online."

"The spaceport has to be completely rebuilt, so it isn't a huge loss if its power supply failed," Hannah returned, a little more aggressively than Rhys expected from her.

Brandon's gaze switched between her and Rhys. Rhys could almost see his enhanced brain trying to figure out the dynamic before him, what he was missing. *What's going on?* he asked via their shared link.

Nothing, Rhys replied.

Your heart rates are elevated.

It's been an exciting day.

Brandon pinned Rhys with a hard stare but didn't comment further. "When should the spaceport repairs begin?" he asked Hannah.

"I'll have to talk about that with everyone else," she

replied. "I know you're all superheroes, but we still have a limited number of resources and labor."

Brandon nodded, gave Rhys another questioning look, and left.

As his footfalls faded down the corridor, Rhys and Hannah stared at each other, both unsure what to do next. Rhys ached to take her back into his arms, but didn't know how that would be received.

"Thank you for turning the power back on," Hannah finally said.

"Technically, you did it."

"You know what I mean. Thank you for repairing the grid and letting me turn on that lever. I appreciate the symbolism."

"You're welcome." He cleared his throat. "Thank you for the kiss."

That blush returned to her cheeks. Rhys liked that he could do that to her. "Oh."

"I haven't kissed anyone before," he added.

Her eyes widened in surprise. "*Oh.*"

An unexpected, unwelcome sense of nervousness washed over him. "May I try again?"

Hannah looked at the control room's open door, then back to Rhys. "Is this going to make things weird?"

"How could a kiss be weird?"

"This could make our working relationship weird," Hannah explained. "We're also sharing my home right now."

Rhys understood. "So, we cannot combine our working relationship with our personal desires."

"Yeah, it could complicate things."

"A kiss could complicate such things?"

"It wouldn't stop at kissing. It never does."

"Of course it could," Rhys pointed out. "We're both in

control of our emotions and impulses. But if you don't want to kiss me, you're under no obligation to."

"You're making this even harder for me, you know?"

"No," Rhys replied, confused. "I don't."

"I want to kiss you," Hannah replied. She swallowed. "Among other things."

Vague, shadowy images of his naked arms and legs twined with a woman filled his mind. Her cries of pleasure encouraged him, her breathy voice repeating his name as he thrust into her in time with the slam of their bed's headboard against the wall. He had no idea who the woman was, but it must have been his original's memory, based on the bed. Beds aboard ships and spaceports didn't have headboards.

He thought about his current iteration doing that, but with Hannah underneath him. It was a heady notion, one that had every nerve in his body alight. The front of his flight trousers became uncomfortably tight.

"Rhys? You faded out again."

"I remembered something," he replied hoarsely.

Concern flared across her features. "Another flashback?"

"Yes, but it wasn't a bad one. The opposite, in fact."

"Do you want to talk about it?"

He shook his head. "It would make things weird."

That remark drew a smile from her. "Was it *that* kind of flashback?"

"Do you mean sexual? Yes."

She laughed. "I appreciate the bluntness."

"What's the point of lying?"

"That's a good attitude to have." Her mirth faded. "Thank you to you and your team for repairing the power grid."

He nodded. "Thank you for letting my people stay on New Eden."

"I'm glad you're here," she said. "And it's not just because of your tech or what you're doing for us."

A warmth that had nothing to do with his warring hormones filled him, and he tried to smile. "I'm glad I met you." More than anything or anyone else, Rhys was glad to have found Hannah. Smart, determined, beautiful Hannah.

She looked like she wanted to say something, but paused. Finally, she said, "I'm going to go back to the agri center." Disappointment welled up in him, but he nodded again in response.

"I'll see you at dinner," he promised.

And until then, he would ruminate over everything that had just happened.

———

HANNAH CONSIDERED SKIPPING the rest of the day and returning home to reflect on the events at the power station. *There was more than one kind of electricity in the air!* In the end, common sense won out. She returned to the agri center. There, she found SP29 and a couple of other cyborgs assembling a machine in the barn. "This is a scaled-down clone pod," SP29 explained by way of greeting.

It took a second for her to switch gears and turn her thoughts back to her job. "This is how you're going to make new chickens!" she exclaimed, fascinated.

"Cows too. Jasmine said she missed cheese and steak." Was Hannah seeing things, or did SP29's features soften when he mentioned Jasmine's name? "Animal cloning will take longer than using sowing enhanced seeds," SP29 continued. "We expect to have chicken embryos ready within the next ten days, and hatched chicks about three weeks after that, assuming their gestation is normal. We've never done this with animals before. It's a little more complicated than growing a human."

"You can't be serious," Hannah protested. "Are you outfitting the chicks with X-ray vision and data ports?"

SP29 grinned. "We are not. But we've never done this before with a chicken, and we want to get this right the first time. No sense in causing a creature to suffer if we can take precautions."

"Good point." Hannah had never considered the finer points of cloning and ethics.

Hannah watched another cyborg attach a plastiglas cover to the pod's top. SP29's last statement reminded her of something she'd been dying to ask a cyborg about, but she didn't know if it was polite or not. SP29 had been more willing to talk about the specifics of being a cyborg and clone than Rhys had, and she thought he might be more receptive to answering her questions. "Can I ask you something?"

"Sure."

"I'm not trying to be rude, and you don't have to answer. Do you ever have memories from your other clones or your original?" A shadow crossed SP29's face. Hannah immediately regretted asking. "I'm sorry," she said.

Just as quickly, it was gone. "Don't be," SP29 replied. "This was going to come up sooner or later. Old memories have been known to resurface for some of us. They're rarely pleasant." His voice dropped. "Walk with me."

Intrigued, Hannah did so. They strode out of the barn and into the sunshine. It was nice to look at the fields and not feel overwhelmed at what needed to be done or be terrified of losing food before it could be harvested.

Lettuce and wheat had been planted, along with a couple other varieties of vegetables she was unfamiliar with but had been assured would be a good match for the New Eden soil. The sight of the tended fields and vegetable patches was a balm to Hannah's soul.

But she wasn't here to gaze on the fields. "What haven't you told me?" she asked. "Is there something I need to know about your people?"

"There's nothing untoward that we've been keeping from you," SP29 replied. "Truthfully, we don't know why we were created in the first place."

"Rhys has said as much."

"We're certain it was for something terrible," SP29 continued. They walked past an herb garden, the smells of basil and rosemary pleasant. "War or terrorism purposes. Some of us have had memories of our originals or itera-tions doing horrific things or horrific things being done to them. I've had a few weird memories resurface since I was cloned."

"Aren't there other cyborgs who've been around long enough to tell you what could've happened to a previous iteration?"

"I'm sure there were, before our predecessors made themselves independent. But we have no records of a cyborg rebellion. We think our previous iterations destroyed them as a means of protection. All of us were grown in clone pods and have been traveling together for the last twenty-eight years."

"You woke up in the pods one day as full-grown adults, and that was that?"

SP29 nodded. "Essentially. We were born with the technical knowledge necessary for space travel, speech skills, all of that. We don't know why."

"And you aren't keen on finding out."

"No. We've kept our trading and interactions with other peoples to a minimum. I'm one of the cyborgs who most easily passes for an organic human, so I was often the one recruited to do that." Another unreadable look crossed his face. "DL16 is the other one who most appears human. He doesn't even have wrist ports. No idea why."

His voice took on an odd, strained note when he mentioned DL16. Hannah recalled that was the other cyborg Jasmine was enamored with. "Have you considered using your original's name?"

"No. I'm not him. I don't want to be him," SP29 replied shortly. "Maybe I'll pick a name later, maybe I won't. I haven't decided yet."

Hannah didn't ask more about his original. "Should I be worried about Rhys?" she asked. "Are his flashbacks and memory resurfacing something to worry about?"

SP29 gave her a look that reminded her of Jasmine's when she'd guessed that Hannah had feelings for her new roommate. "I worry about him," she added. "We're friends. That's what friends do."

"I'm not sure there's anything you could do, except listen to him if he wants to talk about it."

Which Rhys didn't want to do. She sighed. "Thank you for the advice."

"You're welcome. I also wanted to ask you about one of the empty housing blocks."

Hannah sucked in a harsh breath. One of the blocks, on the southern end of New Eden's settlement, was little more than rubble. The houses had been picked over for shreds of anything useful. They were the oldest, dating back to the earliest days of the colonists.

As if SP29 could read her mind, he continued. "The block closest to the power station."

She exhaled in relief. Those houses—which were more

one-room shacks than proper houses—were to the north of the settlement. "That block was abandoned when the former council wanted everyone to live closer together as the population shrank."

"It's only a kilometer and a half away from the main settlement."

"That's a significant distance on a land mass as small as New Eden."

"We think the houses could be restored for our use," SP29 continued. "Would it be all right if we started that, now that the power has been reactivated and the food supply restarted?"

"You don't have to justify wanting your own spaces," Hannah said. "I don't see why you couldn't live in those houses." It pained her to say those words, more than she would ever admit. She liked having Rhys in her house, as closed-off as he could be.

And that kiss. It was far too short, far too gentle, but it was seared into her memory. Part of her wished she had stayed in the power station with him, awkwardness and an open control room door be damned.

SP29 beamed. "Thank you."

They stood in front of the tomato garden. Hannah looked back at the barn. "I should get back to work."

"What for? You're caught up. All we have left to do is clone chickens."

"I should learn how to do that and how the machine works."

"You don't want to take a break?"

"Maybe tomorrow," Hannah replied. If she went home now, all she would be able to think about was Rhys and their interrupted kiss. At least if she stayed at the agri center, she could learn something new.

"You never quit, do you?" But SP29 didn't discourage her. She walked alongside him to the barn.

If she quit, she might think about Rhys. She might think about the quake, about her parents. About how she had lost her ability to relate to other people and could only focus on work.

"No," she replied. "I don't."

Maybe I should.

———

A FEW GRAVES were marked with stones and rough-hewn wooden crosses that were mostly splinters, although most were bereft of monuments. If Hannah wasn't intimately familiar with New Eden's cemetery, she would have assumed there were far fewer people buried there than there were, but she knew it well. The cemetery was now full, thanks to time and the earthquake. Beneath a flat rock on its westernmost side were her parents. She'd found the rock on the ocean's edge a couple of weeks after the quake and had hauled it to the cemetery herself, needing them to have their final resting place marked. She didn't have the means to engrave it with the names Leonard and Tilly Forsyth.

She hadn't even been able to bring them out to the cemetery when she had helped clear away the debris after the community center had collapsed. Jasmine had arranged for their burial, with the help of Freddy and Rhoda Barnes. Jasmine had stuck a little scrap of fabric on their mound, so Hannah could find it later on her own and mark it. Not for the first time, guilt ate at her that she hadn't been able to face her parents one last time.

And she'd hardly visited them after the quake. Today marked the first time in six months that she'd made the trek across the settlement to the cemetery. She didn't have any flowers to lay at their site and felt foolish for not picking a few before she arrived.

"I made contact. We're getting help. We might be okay," she murmured, hoping they could hear her. She sat at the foot of the grave and closed her eyes, trying to . . . meditate, maybe? Pray? Hannah hadn't been raised in an especially spiritual home. She doubted she was capable of believing in the god whose name she so frequently took in vain.

Deliberate footsteps sounded behind her. She didn't have to turn around to know who it was. The memory of their kiss flashed through her mind. "Hello, Rhys."

"Should I leave? Is this a bad time?"

"No, you can stay." She patted the ground next to her. "Sit with me."

He did so, black-clad legs sticking straight out ahead of him. "Your parents?" His voice was uncharacteristically soft.

She nodded and swallowed the lump in her throat. "I guess you can tell we're in a cemetery."

"The grave markers give that away."

"And you can probably sense the people."

"That, too. I was trying to be sensitive."

Despite the grief weighing at her, she couldn't help but smile. "I appreciate that." She fixed her gaze on the flat ocean rock. "They were in the community center when the quake happened. That building was the oldest, and it took the worst hit. No one in there survived after the ceiling came down on them."

"Hannah . . ."

She couldn't keep herself from talking. It was weird; she'd been avoiding thinking about it since she'd hauled the rock over, keeping herself busy harvesting failing crops. "There was supposed to be a big meeting that day about cattle or something. I was running late, otherwise I would've been in there too. Instead, I was on the path when the ground started to shake. I thought it would split open, and I'd fall right through." Her vision went blurry and she realized she was crying. "Half that building was stone. Heavy as shit. The roof was this old heavy material from the old world. I don't know what it was called. But it flattened everyone. They never had a chance."

For a few moments, the only sounds were of Rhys's quiet, measured breaths and her sobs. She appreciated that he wasn't telling her that the quake wasn't her fault or she shouldn't feel guilty for living through it when so many New Edeners hadn't. "I didn't even have the strength to bury them myself," she added. "Jasmine helped with that. I couldn't bring myself to haul them out of the rubble, either."

He still didn't reply, only tentatively reached one of his gloved hands to hers, squeezing her fingers. "Do you visit them often?" he finally asked.

"Not as often as a good daughter should."

"Is there a manual for how the adult children of late parents are supposed to behave?"

The question was so ridiculous that Hannah smiled through her tears. "If there is, it was probably burned as kindling."

Rhys's next words were slow, deliberate. "I can't offer advice or insight on your peoples' bereavement rituals, nor did I know your parents. But wouldn't they be proud of the way you've continued on in the face of continued adversity?"

"I hope they would be."

"I don't fully understand grief," he continued. "But

what I know of it, there isn't a correct way to privately mourn, at least among humanoid cultures."

"Except yours. You regrow your friends."

"Our previous iterations must have grieved for one another before a new clone was generated. I did, when CW43 expired shortly after we were grown together."

"Expired, Rhys? Really?"

He nodded, then shrugged. "Passed away, whichever phrase you prefer."

Curiosity was a distraction from her grief. "Is there a CW44?"

"Yes, he did a great deal of work on the power station."

"Huh." Hannah squeezed his hand back, grateful for the contact. "Thank you."

"For what?"

"Being a sounding board. Being my *friend*," she emphasized. "I'm usually not able to talk about this." She glanced back at the stone. "I think my parents would be happy with what we've done so far." She stood and brushed dirt off her shorts. "Why are you here, anyway?"

"I was looking for you."

Her heart skipped a beat. "Why?"

He looked flummoxed, unable to offer an answer right away. "I just wanted to, is all."

An odd warmth spread her through her chest as she considered his words. "I'm glad you did."

CHAPTER EIGHT

Rʜʏs ʟᴀʏ ɪɴ ʙᴇᴅ, unable to sleep. His sensors told him that it was just past two in the morning and that all of his functions were optimal, which didn't explain why he was lying awake in bed, staring at the ceiling.

He knew the reason, and it wasn't because one of his components was offline. The woman slumbering across the landing, who had been unusually quiet since her visit to the cemetery, was entirely responsible for his sleeplessness.

The squeak of a door's hinges opening had him sitting upright. Subtle creaks in the floorboards, then the stairs, brought an uncharacteristic smile to his face. Perhaps Hannah was as affected as he was.

He debated if he should get out of bed or not for a moment. They needed to talk, he decided, even though neither of them was very good at it. He waited until Hannah reached the first floor before he slipped out of bed and followed her.

Rhys found her in the kitchen, clad in a long sleeveless garment that only reached the tops of her thighs, her hair unbraided, a glass of water in her hand. She glowed in the illumination offered by the ceiling light above their heads. Any words he might have had to say disappeared as he took in the incredible sight. She didn't speak either, instead staring at him.

"I was trying to be stealthy," she finally said.

"My senses are finely honed."

"Yeah, I'd be surprised if they weren't." She set her glass in the sink.

"I couldn't sleep."

"Neither could I," she confessed. "I've been tossing and turning all night."

"I couldn't hear it."

"It's an expression," she explained.

Rhys understood. He cleared his throat. "Do you wish to talk about it?"

She surprised him when she smiled. "I like how direct you are."

"Being anything less wastes time."

She leaned against the counter, crossing her arms under her breasts, which Rhys tried and failed not to notice. "You picked a hell of a time to start a conversation. This is the first time I've ever seen you without gloves, let alone most of your clothes. It's distracting."

"What's special about my gloves?"

"It's your hands I was curious about," she explained. "Jasmine said that SP29 has ports in his."

Was Hannah's interest in him mere curiosity? Was he a novelty? The masculine pride he didn't know he had until recently stung at that idea. "I see."

She immediately picked up on his discomfort. "I don't mean in a circus freak kind of way. You don't have to show me if you don't want to. I'll just stay here and enjoy the rest of the view."

He wore only a pair of loose drawstring trousers. In

addition to the ports in his hands, he also had components embedded in his skin, in his chest and back, but he didn't think that was what Hannah was admiring. An uncharacteristic surge of confidence swelled in him at her notice.

At least they were talking. "I'll show you."

She padded to where he stood, and he obediently held out his hands. The ports were small, barely raised ridges along his fingertips, with larger ones in his wrists. She touched the ports, sending sparks across his skin and his heart rate skyrocketing. He inhaled sharply. Without letting him go, she said, "I don't see how this isn't going to complicate things."

"I'm certain we can find a solution that will work for both of us."

"I've been thinking about how we shouldn't be having these feelings," she said.

"Aren't we both adults? I was last cloned twenty-eight years ago. You aren't much younger than I am."

"Twenty-six. Thank you for noticing." She gave him a wry smile. "I was thinking about feelings and attraction and how it's unlikely that all of our people are going to be living like monks now that you're here." She took a deep breath and traced her thumb on the back of his hand. He had no idea such a small touch could feel that intimate. "I'm sure there will be plenty of New Edeners and cyborgs hooking up before the month is out. Probably sooner. So, I'm not going to fight this. I like you."

Hope flared to life in him, warring with the desire he felt when he was in her presence. "I like you too."

He caught her gaze and held it. He wrapped her hands in his, then leaned forward to kiss her.

She gasped against his lips before she reciprocated. He instinctively opened his mouth, and she took that as the invitation it was, her tongue touching his. Rhys's knees went weak, quickly corrected by his cybernetics. Arousal thrummed through his body in a steady beat, a primal urge that had him wanting to pick her up bodily and carry her up the stairs to his bedroom.

She gently took his lower lip between her teeth, a gesture he wouldn't have thought to have found erotic. His cock strained against his trousers, and he wondered what it would feel like to have Hannah's hands on him, her mouth. The idea nearly made him spend right in her kitchen.

He broke their kiss, pulling away before he embarrassed himself. He had never had sexual contact before, but he was familiar with the act, knew he was supposed to have more control. When he looked at Hannah, he saw her eyes were half-lidded, her lips swollen. Her nipples were outlined in the thin garment she wore, and he yearned to pull it off her.

"Wow," she said. "You're good at that."

You're a quick study. Hadn't she said that the night before? He pushed aside the otherwise unpleasant memory those words brought out, focusing on the sight in front of him. "I had to stop," he murmured.

"Too intense?" She gave a knowing look at his groin.

He nodded.

"We don't have to do anything you don't want to do," she said softly. "We could just kiss and explore each other. No pressure at all."

Rhys couldn't think of anything better in that moment. "Should we go to your bedroom or mine?"

"Mine," she said automatically. "You're in my parents' room."

"Would that be weird?" he asked.

"Very."

She grabbed his hand and led him out of the kitchen and up the stairs.

———

HANNAH TURNED on the wall lamp next to her bedroom door. She climbed into bed and held the covers open for Rhys. "Room for one more."

He hesitated for half a second before sliding in next to her. He took up most of the bed, and she shifted onto her side. This time, he was the aggressor, his lips meeting hers and hands reaching to rest on her hips and pull her closer to him. Goosebumps popped up along her skin, and she was very aware that only thin material separated them. Her hand slid along his shoulder, over his chest to his stomach, causing his breath to stutter.

Her fingers stilled. "Should I stop?"

"No," he murmured against her lips. He shifted, one hand moving to rest against her hair.

Hannah dared to slide her hand lower, resting it at his navel. His whole body felt as taut as a wire, like he was ready to snap at any moment. Their gazes met, her brown eyes locking on to his, the irises a mechanical gray. The ports in his fingers lightly scraped against her skin where he held on to her, a touch she hadn't known she would like until now.

"Hannah." His voice was rough, a mixture of lust and shame. "I don't know what to do next."

Her heart ached for him. "It's okay. Just tell me what feels good."

His hand covered hers on his stomach. "There," he said. "That feels good." His other hand squeezed her hip. "This too."

She grinned. "I'm thinking we're on the same page."

"I want to see you," he said almost shyly. His fingers plucked at her nightshirt. "May I?"

Hannah nodded. Now, it was her turn to feel a little

self-conscious; no one had seen her without clothes in years, and her body had changed. She was leaner, harder where she once had curves. She straightened enough to grip her shirt's hem and toyed with it for a second, hesitating.

Rhys gave her a hungry look, bolstering her confidence. She pulled it over her head and exhaled shakily.

He stared at her for a moment, looking like he was a man lost in the desert and she was a long-awaited oasis. "You're so beautiful," he breathed.

"You're not so shabby yourself." She recalled Jasmine's statement about wanting to climb her cyborg roommate "like a tree," and bit back a smile at the memory. She fully understood the sentiment. His body was flawless, the components embedded in his skin only enhancing the effect.

His erection strained against his trousers, a testament to the effect she had on him. It was a heady, powerful feeling. She was curious about what that would feel like, but she kept her hand on his belly, measuring his quick, shallow breaths.

Rhys reached for her, fingertips grazing over her shoulder, to her collarbone, to the swell of her breast. Hannah shivered, surprised that such a featherlight touch could affect her so . Encouraged, he cupped her breast, drawing a mewl from her. It was a terrible tease.

She kissed him again, and his hand moved to cup her head. His tongue swept into her mouth, sending her pulse thrumming and senses on fire. She slipped her hand a little lower on his belly until it grazed his waistband, and he surprised her by covering it with his own and placing it over his erection. She gently stroked him through the fabric, a motion that had him thrusting into her hand and moaning against her lips.

He let her go long enough to push his trousers over his hips, freeing his cock. Hannah met his gaze again, seeking permission, and he raised his hips again, giving it. She wrapped her hand around him and experimentally slid it up and down. "Like that," he breathed, his voice a hoarse, pained whisper. "Please."

Hannah did so, watching his emotions play out on his face as she stroked him and slowly increased her pressure. He directed her, grasping her hand over his and sliding it up and down, his eyes never leaving her face. With his other hand, he grasped her breast, rolling and pinching her nipple between his fingers. A jolt of pure pleasure shot through her—where the hell had he learned to do that?

The motion had her arching her back and wishing she could straddle him, have him fill that aching spot that demanded it. But she stayed where she was. This was all about him tonight.

He came with a groan, grabbing her head and pulling her in for a kiss as he spasmed under her hand. His breath was harsh and labored, as if he had just run a marathon. Hannah rested her head on his chest, listening to his heart beat a rapid tattoo against his ribs. "That was incredible," he said. He pressed a kiss to the top of her head. "Thank you."

Before she could say anything else, he got out of bed and went to the bathroom. He'd cleaned up when he returned and had a towel for her hand. "You don't have to thank me," she said. "I wanted to do it."

"It seemed polite." He cleared his throat. "Should I return to my bed?"

It would be so easy for her to say yes. Part of her wanted to, not wanting to make things more complicated than they already were, but Hannah suspected it was too late for that.

But her heart, the illogical thing that it was, wanted him to stay with her. Hadn't she already told him that she wanted to be with him? "No, of course not." It might have been her imagination, but she thought Rhys's shoulders sagged in relief, just a little.

He switched off the light and slid back into bed. She settled against his chest. "Do you think you'll be able to sleep now?" he asked into her hair.

She smiled. "Yes."

"Shall I reciprocate?"

It was the most formal sexual invitation she'd ever received, yet it still did *things* to her. Lascivious images filled her mind, and she almost agreed. "Tonight was for you," she said, raising her head to meet his eyes. They shone with an otherworldly light in the dark. "We'll worry about me another time."

"I have had resurfaced memories of my original when he . . ."

"Rhys, do *not* tell me about that. I won't talk about my past experiences, and you don't have to tell me about your original's."

His arms tightened around her. "I don't like to think about you with other people," he muttered.

"There's only been one, and I haven't been with anyone in a very long time. There's no one else right now."

"Is it irrational that I only want to be with you?"

"No," she replied. "I lean toward monogamy, myself."

He reached for her jaw and lightly swept his fingers along it, as if reassuring himself that she was still there. He tilted up her chin to kiss her. "I think I do too," he said. "Good night, Hannah."

———

RHYS THOUGHT there might be no better way to wake up in the morning than next to a naked Hannah. Her head rested against his shoulder, unbound hair draped across his arm and chest.

If he was an organic human and unequipped with his memory banks, he might have thought last night was a dream. He would treasure the images that still raced through his mind for the rest of his life.

Not wanting to wake her, he shifted, but it was for naught. "Mm?" she murmured, raising her head. The bedsheet slipped down, revealing the swells of her breasts. Rhys's mouth went dry at the sight.

"Good morning," he said. A wave of shyness crested over him, which was ridiculous, considering all they had shared. He cleared his throat. "Did you sleep well?"

"Yeah." She sounded surprised to admit that. She blinked, her eyes widening at the sight of him still naked. "I think I could get used to that."

Rhys warmed at her words. "I think I could too." Not knowing what else to say, he changed the subject. "I'm going to start working on restoring the launch site today, now that the power grid is back online."

"Oh, wow. That's a huge job. I don't think the equipment needed to fix all that can even be found on New Eden."

He shrugged. "You managed to transmit an SOS."

"And the broadcast equipment failed right after I sent it. I rebuilt it with melted spoons. It was sheer dumb luck that I managed to do that much."

"We can leave New Eden for necessary supplies," Rhys pointed out. "There are enough trading depots nearby that doing so wouldn't be an issue."

That caught Hannah's attention. "How close?"

"The nearest waystation would take three to five days'

travel time to arrive, depending on ship speeds. This area of space is prone to ion storms, so there's a possibility of delays."

Hannah stared at him, aghast. "Are you telling me that civilization has only been a few days away all this time?"

Rhys didn't know if he'd said something wrong. "Yes?"

"Goddamn it!" She threw herself back against the pillows and pounded her fists into the blankets. She glanced at him. "This wasn't directed at you. It's for my idiot ancestors. We don't even have a fucking proper *hospital* here, and medical equipment and all of that has only been a couple of days' spaceflight away all this time?"

Rhys took a seat on the bed next to her. Tears had gathered in her eyes and she squeezed them shut. "Hannah, you don't have to live like that anymore. We can obtain anything your planet needs."

"*Our* planet," she corrected him.

He liked that she said that. "Yes. We also have ways of purchasing these items."

"I hadn't even considered the money aspect." She covered her face in her hands. "I'm really bad at this."

He pulled them away. "You are not. I do think it would be prudent to call a meeting at the amphitheater. We will have to discuss travel schedules and supply lists."

He didn't let go of her hands and she didn't pull away. Instead, their eyes locked on each other. Something in the room shifted, as palpable as an incoming storm, and Rhys was again aware that they were both still undressed. Her nipples tented the thin bedsheet, and her breath came a little faster. So did Rhys's. He leaned over and kissed her, putting everything he could into it, hoping he pleased her as much as she'd pleased him the night before. She made a whimpering noise against his lips, so he supposed he did. A surge of pride and lust welled in him that he could do that.

Her upper body shifted, back arching as though she wanted to be closer to him. With shaking fingers, he reached for the sheet separating their bodies and slipped it down. Guided by an instinct he hadn't known he possessed, his mouth kissed a path down her throat, past her collarbones, to her breast, ready to take one nipple into his mouth. Hannah gasped beneath him, her hands fisting in his hair, encouraging him to go lower. Her grip sent anticipation thrumming through him as the possibilities of what could come next flew through his mind.

A knock at the front door had both of them frozen in place on the bed. Rhys met Hannah's surprised gaze. "What the fuck?" she whispered.

"We could ignore it," Rhys said.

"I like the way you're thinking." Another knock, more insistent this time, sounded through the house. "But whoever it is won't go away until I talk to them." She climbed out of bed, leaving Rhys on top of the covers. She let out a small sigh as she picked up a worn robe, tying its sash around her waist. "Poor Rhys. You're in quite a state." She gave a pointed look at his erection. It nearly hurt.

Suddenly feeling a little shy, Rhys cleared his throat. "It's a testament to you."

She laughed, then leaned over and kissed him. "I think that's the hottest thing anyone's ever said to me."

Rhys kissed her back, the realization that it was the first time he'd ever seen her laugh hitting him hard. He thought he might've just seen a glimpse of the old Hannah, the woman she was before her planet was plunged into chaos. He wanted to see more of her. "I have other, more explicit platitudes as well."

"Keep them coming." She ran a hand through her tangled hair. "Actually, wait until I see whoever is at the door and send them away." Before she left the bedroom, she added, "Don't come downstairs unless you're dressed. I don't want to make this a thing for gossip just yet." With that admonishment, she left, footsteps echoing down the creaky stairs.

Rhys tried not to let that statement sting as much as it did, true as it was. Revealing their physical relationship, brand-new as it was, would only muddy the relationship between his people and the New Edeners. It was easier for everyone this way.

Still naked, he crept over to the doorway and listened to the conversation playing out at Hannah's front door. A man's voice had started rising in volume as he vented his frustrations about a house. Rhys's memory banks matched the voice to the face of an older man named Ollie, the one who was so upset about cyborgs living on New Eden.

"There are four of them in my uncle's house!" Ollie said.

"You've already told me that, and I knew it, anyway, after the billeting arrangements were decided," Hannah replied wearily. "I'm not sure why we're having this conversation at this time in the morning."

"It's half-past nine, and frankly, I'm surprised you're still lying around in your pajamas."

Rhys's ire rose at the man's impudence.

"Everyone's entitled to sleep in once in a while," Hannah said sharply. "And not that I need to clear this with you, but today, I'm going to be looking into repairing the spaceport."

Rhys's ears strained to hear the sound of Ollie's enraged breathing. "Why the hell would you do that?"

Hannah's voice rose in anger. "Why the hell wouldn't I do that? We don't have a *hospital*, Ollie! We don't have any medication! We were a dying people before the earthquake ever happened!"

"Listen here, young lady. If you think I'm going to stand back and watch as you destroy what our ancestors created, I have some news for . . ."

"Oh, shut up." Rhys bit back a smile as he heard Ollie's gasp. "Our ancestors were fucking idiots, and if we keep trying to live as they did, we're going to die out in a couple of years. There's a big galaxy out there. We need their help. Living like this isn't sustainable anymore."

"It would be, if . . ."

Hannah cut him off again. "If what? You do realize we didn't have the strength or technology to bring the power grid back online, and it's not like you've actually done anything to help out since the quake."

Rhys leaned over the railing, wishing he was downstairs to see the old man's expression as Hannah laid into him.

"You sit in your house, waiting for food to be delivered to you, then complain when it's nothing but carrots and eggs!" she shouted. "You show up to community meetings and whine about not having electricity. You've done nothing but complain since the quake. You didn't even help with the cleanup outside of your own fucking yard." Ollie made a noise, as if to protest, but Hannah forged on. "You've contributed nothing since the earthquake happened. You didn't even help bury the dead. You didn't even *lose* anyone in the quake, yet you refuse to help anyone who did."

"I cannot believe . . ."

"That I'm speaking to you this way? Believe it, and get the fuck off my property." The door squeaked on its hinges. "And don't come around here in the morning again. It's weird." With that, she slammed the door.

Rhys was only too eager to descend the stairs as soon as the lock was pulled across the door. Hannah leaned against it and rubbed her temples. "Fucking Ollie," she muttered. She looked up, the worry lines between her brows smoothing out. "Wow. I guess cyborgs don't have any hangups about modesty."

"I don't when I'm with you."

She tilted her head to the side, a smile on her face. "You really have a knack for saying romantic things that I never expected to be romantic."

Rhys was only too happy to take her back into his arms. She leaned into him and breathed deeply. "You smell good," she said into his shoulder.

He kissed the top of her head. "So do you." His arms tightened around her. "You don't have to go to the spaceport today," he said, changing the subject. "You need some rest."

"And I will get some rest after you and some of your cyborg buddies have assessed the damage to the spaceport," she said. "That's the last big existing infrastructure project we have to tackle." She sighed. "We also need a proper hospital. The old medical clinic was destroyed in the quake."

"We should also establish a seismic activity monitoring center at some point."

"Yeah, I don't want to go through this again."

Rhys wanted to ask about the quake, get some more specifics about where it occurred, but he knew she wasn't up for that yet. Might not be for months. Besides that, Hannah had enough to worry about without delving into her trauma before she was ready to do so.

She pulled away from him, determination on her face. He ignored his body's protestations at the broken contact. "All right," she said. "I'm getting ready for the day. Could you call some of the other cyborgs, and we'll take a look at the spaceport?"

He wanted to go back to bed with her, see what else he

could remember from the original Rhys's sexual repertoire, but he forced himself to nod. "I would like to do that as well," he lied.

She looked like she didn't believe him, but didn't question his answer. "I won't be long."

CHAPTER NINE

The meeting was going better than Hannah thought it would. Nervousness about announcing the rebuilding of the spaceport had her palms damp with sweat and her stomach in knots as she stood on the amphitheater's stage, New Edeners and cyborgs at attention.

"I'm sure most of us agree that our old way of life is no longer sustainable," Hannah said. "The infrastructure repairs and tech the cyborgs brought with them will only delay the inevitable by another year or two, at the most. It's time for New Eden to join intergalactic society and establish interplanetary trading and communications."

A murmur of agreement rose through the crowd, setting her mind at ease. She glanced at Rhys, who stood a meter or so away from her. He gave her the barest of nods, his lips upturned in a ghost of an encouraging smile. The small gesture made her stomach flip-flop in a way she did *not* need right now, and she felt herself blush. She hoped no one else noticed.

"Who the hell put you in charge?"

Irritation flared in her at the sound of Ollie's voice.

The memory of his banging on her front door, interrupting what she'd hoped would be a continuation of the previous night's activities with Rhys, had her balling her hands into fists at her side. "Haven't we had this conversation before?" she snapped. "No one's specifically in charge at this point."

"Hannah's done the most work out of all of us." Jasmine's voice rang out over the crowd. "How many times do we have to remind you of that?"

"I just think, if we held a democratic election like we did before . . ."

"Who the hell else is going to run? You?" Jasmine countered. She straightened in her seat and turned around to scan the crowd. Her gaze locked on Ollie's. "You spend all day in your house, waiting for people to bring shit to you, and only leave to complain. We've been dying off even before the quake, and I'm sure all of us would've been dead within five years if the cyborgs hadn't shown up. Hannah's right. This isn't sustainable."

Jasmine caught Hannah's eye and nodded in approval. Hannah released a breath she hadn't realized she was holding. "It isn't a scary universe out there," she said. She turned to Rhys. "Right?"

"Well, of course, we would only be working with peaceful people," he said.

"And they're peaceful in this part of the universe, *right*?" she pressed. She tried to convey to him through her expression that this was the only way they would be able to get people on board with interplanetary communication and trade.

His eyes widened slightly, and she thought he might've picked up on the hint. "Oh, yes. New Eden is very remote, but the closest colonies and planets are friendly."

"What's the estimated window for the spaceport's

repair?" asked Rodelle, speaking up for the first time. Her voice held a note of confidence that hadn't been there since her husband had died.

"The damage is extensive," Rhys replied. "All of the components are badly outdated, and many are unsalvageable. The spaceport's control tower can be renovated into a workable state within the next few weeks, but the launch pad will require thermo-protective materials that can't be sourced on New Eden. The lack of thermo-protection is why we haven't taken off for other colonies to source them. We thought it best to acquire as much as we can in one trip, to reduce the environmental damage our ship would cause for takeoffs and landings in your meadow. We're still making an inventory of what we need."

"What about training?" Rodelle asked. "New Edeners should know how to control the spaceport, not just the cyborgs."

"Absolutely," Rhys replied. "We think it would be best if people volunteered to help us rebuild for that reason, so they become more comfortable with the technology."

"Can we go with you into space?" Jasmine asked excitedly. A murmur of similar questions soon followed. Hannah gave her own hopeful look at Rhys.

Rhys glanced at the other cyborgs, who nodded. "We don't see why not. If you feel you're capable of safe space travel, you're welcome to join us on supply runs."

"This will end badly!" Ollie shouted.

"Fuck off, Ollie!" snapped Jasmine.

"Our ancestors . . ."

"Our ancestors were full of shit!" yelled Jasmine. "My God, how many times do we have to go over this?" She stood up and turned around. "I'm tired of people dying of diseases that can be cured with a pill or spray! I'm sick of constantly wondering if there's going to be another earthquake and we won't know in time!" Her voice had risen to a fever pitch, bordering on hysterical. Alarm flared through Hannah; she'd never seen her friend like this before.

"Our lives are awful like this!" she screamed. "If you want to rot away in your house and refuse to join the modern universe, you go right fucking ahead, Ollie! But the rest of us want to have a chance at living a normal span of years and making something of ourselves!"

Rage colored Ollie's face red, and he opened his mouth to offer a rebuttal. Before he could, Rodelle said, "This is not the time," she said icily.

"When is the time?" Ollie asked.

"Never," replied Rodelle. "The old way of life is behind us, thank God, and I don't think anyone wants to hear you whine about it." Her voice caught, and she took a couple of breaths, fortifying herself. Her next words were even, almost clipped in her anger. "I'd like to remind some of the people gathered here that the quake's death toll wouldn't have been so high if we'd had access to medical care and the infrastructure was in good repair." She returned to her seat.

Hannah thought about her parents, who might have survived the disaster had the community center been quake-proof. She swallowed the lump in her throat that the memory always brought. "There are a million other reasons this has to happen," she said. She looked at the sea of faces, so many of them wearing hopeful expressions for the first time in years. Not just hope, she realized. People were *happy* again.

"How long will this take?" someone asked.

Rhys took a deep breath, then started listing an estimated timeline for the spaceport's construction, and Hannah relaxed for a moment, grateful to have the spotlight off her. He'd lost a little of the stiffness and awkwardness he had when his people first landed, answering questions with a more human confidence.

Had he found that with her the night before? She bit back a smile at the memory as a flush suffused her body. The feeling was tainted by the knowledge that the reason things hadn't progressed earlier in the day was because of Ollie being a bastard again. She hoped no one noticed her blush.

"Unless there's something Hannah would like to discuss?" The mention of her name from Rhys's lips pulled her back into reality.

Damn it, people were looking at her expectantly. What had Rhys just said? "Sorry, could you repeat that?" she asked, hoping no one else noticed her being flustered.

Rhys's voice was calm and level. "Is the meeting adjourned? Is there anything else we should talk about while everyone's still assembled?"

Hannah glanced at the crowd, noting Jasmine's curious expression. Next to her, Rodelle also had a quizzical look on her face. Had they noticed something between her and Rhys, picked up on that connection between them? Knowing Jasmine, it was very possible. She knew Hannah better than anyone.

"I can't think of anything," Hannah replied. "Although, if anyone has anything else they want to discuss, you know where to find me." She thought about Ollie's interruption. "Just check in with me at a reasonable hour," she added. She threw a glare in Ollie's direction for good measure.

The crowd slowly dispersed. Rhys hopped off the stage with a grace that belied his size and held out a hand for Hannah. Despite his stoic expression, there was a warmth in his eyes, a look meant only for her. Her heart fluttered for a couple of beats when his gloved hand touched her skin.

"Are you all right?" he murmured when she was safely on the ground.

"Why wouldn't I be?"

"Your cardiovascular rate . . ."

"Is fine," she whispered. She nearly said, *It's nothing*, but that would've been a lie. It was entirely because of him.

"It's increased," he protested, his voice still quiet. Hannah appreciated his discretion.

"Stop being so hot, and my heart rate will go back to normal."

Understanding dawned on his face. "I see."

He was still holding her hand. The sensation didn't register to Hannah until the contact was broken. She already missed it.

"Hannah."

She squeezed her eyes shut at the sound of Jasmine's voice. She already knew what her friend had just seen. "Hey," she said, forcing levity into her tone. She gave Jasmine what she hoped was a bright smile.

There wasn't a trace of judgment on Jasmine's face—Hannah suspected she was incapable of it—but there was definitely curiosity. "Are you doing anything now?" Jasmine asked.

"I was going to go to the spaceport," Hannah began, but Rhys cut her off.

"There won't be a lot for you to do at the spaceport today," he said. "Some of us are going to evaluate the damage and make a list of supplies and repairs. You're still welcome to join us today, of course."

"Take the rest of the day off," Jasmine urged. "You deserve it. The power's on and the food supply is secure again. Hang out with me and Rodelle for a couple of hours."

Hannah glanced over Jasmine's shoulder. Rodelle was speaking with her sister-in-law, Lorena. Rodelle gave them a nod in their direction while she tried to excuse herself. "Rodelle needs human interaction," Jasmine whispered. Hannah thought about the cyborg living in Rodelle's home and hoped it wasn't going too badly.

Rodelle joined them, and the three walked back to Jasmine's house. It was a surreal feeling, spending time with friends in a social setting instead of gathering together to discuss how to increase agricultural production.

Once inside, Jasmine dramatically closed the door and said, "What's going on?"

"Nothing untoward," Hannah responded.

"That's the stupidest non-answer I've ever heard." Jasmine kicked off her sandals and strode to the kitchen barefoot. "Let me get some wine, and then I'll wheedle it out of you."

Rodelle and Hannah followed. "I meant it when I said there's nothing untoward going on," Hannah protested.

"I'm sure you did. But I need to know the details of how this is going, toward-wise." She uncorked a bottle of dandelion wine and poured some into three mismatched cups. She nodded her head at the small, scarred wooden table in the middle of the kitchen. "Sit." Rodelle and Hannah did so, opposite each other on the benches on either side of the table. Jasmine sat next to Rodelle, giving Hannah the distinct impression that she was about to be interrogated.

All of them looked at each other, not speaking. It reminded Hannah of the staring contests she and Jasmine had when they were kids. Finally, she said, "Don't say anything to anyone."

"Of course we won't," Jasmine said, affronted. "When have I ever blabbed about anything secret?"

"I know, but things are different now."

"Rodelle won't say anything, either. Politicians' wives are used to keeping secrets."

"Jackson was hardly a statesman. He mostly broke up fights about livestock." Rodelle had a faraway look on her face, as she did whenever she spoke about Jackson, but her eyes were dry. In fact, she was wearing a long yellow tunic Hannah knew to to be her favorite, and a loose pair of shorts instead of the threadbare pajamas she had worn since Jackson died. Her long dark blond hair neatly arranged in a braid that wound around her head. Rodelle looked more put together than she had since before the quake. A few years older than them, Rodelle used to babysit Hannah and Jasmine when they were children.

The mention of Jackson reminded Hannah that some kind of election needed to be held soon, but she didn't bring it up. "Remember what we talked about with you and SP29?" Hannah asked.

Jasmine gave her a look that clearly questioned her intelligence. "Yeah." Turning to Rodelle, she said, "It's only a matter of time before we start banging the cyborgs."

Rodelle nodded. "I'm sure it's already happening." She gave Hannah a sly look.

"It isn't like that," Hannah protested. Although it wasn't for lack of trying. A wave of protectiveness crested over her when she thought about Rhys and what they'd shared. "Some stuff happened between us, is all. It took both of us by surprise." She sipped her wine and tried not to make a face at the taste, which was more bitter than usual. "How are things going with SP29 and DL16?" she asked Jasmine pointedly.

"Nothing's happening. I would've told you if there

was."

"Do you have designs on your housemate?" Rodelle asked Jasmine, surprised. "And someone else?"

"I gave the idea to Hannah. I guess you . . ." Jasmine trailed off. "Never mind."

"I guess you what?" Rodelle took a cautious sip of wine. Her lips thinned. Hannah hoped it was because of the taste and not the question Jasmine had nearly asked.

"Nothing."

"You can finish your question. If you're wondering if I'm pining after my cyborg billet, the answer is no. Asking me about it won't offend me." Rodelle took another drink from her wine before setting the cup on the tabletop.

Jasmine's shoulder slumped in relief. "I'm still sorry."

"Don't be." Rodelle tented her fingers on the table and steered the conversation back to Hannah. "What's going on with your housemate?"

She was unsure how to answer, not being certain of that herself. "I don't think either of us knows," Hannah admitted. "I know saying something is complicated is a cop-out, but it is." She thought about Rhys's total lack of experience but didn't mention it. Even to people she trusted, that information wasn't hers to share. "We've kissed," she admitted. She didn't elaborate further.

"He looks at you like you're the only person in the world," Jasmine said dreamily.

"He does?" She had been too preoccupied with announcements and reactions to notice, not that she wanted to stare at him with stars in her eyes and out them to everyone. Neither of them were ready for that. She had no idea what their relationship could even be called.

"I don't think you'll be able to keep this secret very long," Rodelle said. "Pauline Atwater and one of the cyborgs in the big empty house on the west side are already sleeping together. AL14 or someone, I can't remember his designation."

"How the hell do you know that?" Hannah asked.

"Just because I've been wallowing in my own misery these last couple of years doesn't mean I don't hear things," Rodelle replied.

"Grieving," Jasmine corrected her. "You've been grieving. No one blames you for that."

Rodelle didn't argue with her. "Lorena lives a couple of houses down from Pauline. She told me. They aren't being subtle about it."

"Damn. Good for them," said Jasmine appreciatively. To Hannah, she said, "Good for you two, too."

"I don't know what we are," Hannah protested.

"You have lots of time to figure that out."

Hannah steered the conversation away from Rhys. "The reaction to the news about interplanetary travel was well taken, wasn't it? I only saw the usual suspects complaining about it."

"It was mostly Ollie West, anyway," Jasmine said. "The Barneses whined about it a little, but they shut up when you mentioned establishing a hospital. I think almost everyone's on board who can be convinced that this is a good thing." She took a deep swallow of wine. "This has gone off."

"Yeah, we know," Hannah replied. Rodelle nodded.

"Ugh. Maybe we can get some good booze once we've started trading." She stood up and collected the bottle, pouring it down the sink. "Hannah, have you considered taking Rhys on a date or something?"

"Where would we go?"

"Like for a picnic or something. You could take him to the falls. How much of New Eden has any of the cyborgs seen since they arrived? They've done nothing but work."

How much had Hannah seen of her own planet recently? Once upon a time, she'd loved whiling away the hours wandering around one of New Eden's waterfalls. She recalled it with detachment, as if it had been an anecdote told to her offhand by an acquaintance instead of her lived memory. "That's not a terrible idea," she said slowly.

"Stop worrying about what other people might think about it, and do something together that isn't about the power station or agri center. It isn't normal to have dates in a barn," Jasmine added.

"Both of us would prefer to be discreet," Hannah protested. "We thought it could be a conflict of interest."

"How the hell is that a conflict of interest? There's hardly anyone on New Eden, in the grand scheme of things, and you've already said you don't want to be a leader. You can live your life now." Jasmine's voice softened. "Things are going to get better for everyone, finally. You don't have to skulk around your house in secret if you don't want to."

Hannah considered Jasmine's words. "You're right," she said.

"Of course I am." Jasmine opened a cabinet and picked out another bottle of wine. "More?"

"Oh, no, thank you." Rodelle shuddered.

"I wish you'd said something about the bad bottle."

"I don't drink often enough to know how dandelion wine is supposed to taste."

"Hannah?" Jasmine held out a bottle.

"What the hell. Why not?"

Jasmine smiled and opened the bottle, pouring it into their cups. "Don't worry about what other people might think. All of this—" She waved her arm around. "All of this will work out."

CHAPTER TEN

With Jasmine's words of encouragement in mind, Hannah set about packing a light supper for a picnic. A walk through the falls and food, she decided. That seemed like a good way to get through to a partially cybernetic heart.

"What's this?" Rhys asked when he arrived home and spotted Hannah's family's beat-up picnic basket waiting in the foyer.

Home. It would hurt when housing was repaired, new homes built, and Rhys moved into one. Hannah pushed aside that impending event and smiled. "I thought I could show you the waterfalls," she said. "New Eden's full of them."

To her surprise, Rhys's lips thinned. "Our sensors picked that up when our ship landed."

"There's one spot that's my favorite," Hannah continued. "I haven't been there much since the quake, and I'd like to show it to you. There's also a warm spring you can swim in."

"Swim?" Was it her imagination, or did Rhys look slightly green at the prospect?

She tried not to feel hurt at his reaction. "You don't have to if you don't want to."

He blinked. "I don't have a swimming ensemble."

"What did you use when you drained the power station's bulkheads?" He blanched at the mention of the power station, and she knew she'd hit a sore spot. Did something happen there that he didn't want to talk about? "You don't have to swim," she added. "I can do that enough for both of us."

"My trousers are waterproof and quick-drying. That's what I wore in the flooded bulkheads," Rhys said.

He didn't look convinced that making a trip out to the falls was a good idea. Hannah tamped down her hurt and tried to keep her voice bright. "We don't have to go," she said. "We could enjoy it in the backyard."

"No," he replied sharply. He closed his eyes and took a deep breath. When he spoke again, his voice had softened. "I'd like to see this area that's special to you. I've never seen waterfalls before."

Hannah picked up the basket. Without a word, Rhys took it from her.

I could get used to this. Part of her thought she already was.

"I thought we could talk too," Hannah said. She closed the door behind her, not bothering to lock it. No one did in New Eden. "We've hardly talked about anything but the power station and how much our tech sucks."

"You said you wanted to swim," Rhys said, sidestepping her suggestion. "Where's your swimsuit?"

"I don't bother with one."

Rhys's eyebrows raised. "I see. How far away is this waterfall?"

———

ANXIETY LANDED in his gut like a leaden weight at the thought of being near all that rushing water. The logical part of his brain said it wouldn't be like the bulkhead, that any swimming hole an unenhanced human used would have a bottom he could see. There wouldn't be the pressure of thousands of kilograms of water pressing on his body at all sides. There would be sunlight, warm water, and hopefully a very naked Hannah. That part cheered him up considerably.

She'd gone to so much trouble for him, preparing this meal. He didn't want to disappoint her.

While they walked and before he could be distracted, he said, "We could have the spaceport operational within a month."

Hannah stopped dead in her tracks. "Are you serious?"

"Very. Why would I joke about such a thing?"

"I'm surprised, in a very good way, is all." She picked up the pace again.

They'd cleared her neighborhood and walked along the dusty road that led to the power station. Beyond it were the waterfalls that dotted New Eden's landscape. The sound of rushing water from the main waterfall that powered the planet could be heard from this distance. The low, steady hum of electricity growled as they walked past the building, the volume at a level only cyborgs could hear. It reminded Rhys of the engines aboard his ship.

Hannah reached for his free hand. "May I?" she asked.

He looked down at her small hand wound around his, her suntanned flesh against his black gloves a sharp contrast. It was a gesture of affection, he recalled. One of the original Rhys's memories resurfaced, of walking along a beach, a scantily dressed redheaded woman at his side, fingers intertwined with his.

Rhys recreated that now. As he did so, his heart rate, previously spiking at the thought of being near water again, returned to normal.

"I visited with Jasmine and Rodelle today," Hannah said. "Jasmine already guessed that something's going on between us."

Rhys wasn't sure how he felt about that. "Oh?"

"She said you look at me like I'm the only person in the world," she said shyly. "She picked up on it quickly. I'm not upset about it if you aren't."

"I thought we agreed that this could appear as a conflict of interest." He gently squeezed her hand, trying to convey in that small gesture that he wasn't put out by the news.

"We talked about that too. How would this appear as a conflict of interest in our case? It's not like either of us are in positions where we can be bribed, and as soon as I'm able, I'm stepping away from the leadership role everyone else has put me in." She took a deep breath. "It's also only a matter of time before anyone who wants to hook up with a New Edener will do so. It's already happening. Rodelle's sister-in-law's neighbor started sleeping with a cyborg in the west side rooming house almost immediately."

That was news to Rhys. "How?"

She snorted. "I imagine the usual way."

"I mean, how did that happen without me knowing?"

"Geez, Rhys. Some things are meant to be private. I didn't go into detail about us with Jasmine and Rodelle."

"No, our broadcast link," Rhys patiently explained. "We can communicate that way. It's like an electronic telepathy." Come to think of it, he hadn't heard any of his fellow cyborgs' thoughts in days. It was as if everyone had severed their link to their common network. "Huh."

"Huh, what?"

"No one has spoken that way in a while," Rhys said.

"You're reclaiming your humanity in more ways than one," Hannah said.

They were past the power station, now walking through a dense green forest. A thin path wound through it, and Hannah led him along. "We're almost there," she said happily.

Ten minutes later, they stood in a clearing. A small waterfall, perhaps six meters high, poured into a pool of clear water. Sunlight peeked through the heavy green canopy overhead, dappling the path and reflecting off the pool. Rhys relaxed a little. This, he could handle.

She picked a spot near the pool and took the basket from him. Flipping open the lid, she pulled out a thin blanket made of scrap pieces of fabric and spread it out on the ground. When she sat on it, he followed suit. She handed him a wooden box with a woven reed top and handle that held a couple of sandwiches and handed one to him. She took another for herself.

"Do you not like water?" Hannah asked. "I've never asked you that, and I probably should have. You've been on edge since I suggested we come here."

Rhys paused, his sandwich halfway to his mouth. He didn't want to lie to her. "I didn't do very well when the power station's bulkheads were drained."

"Do you want to talk about it?"

He hesitated, mulling over her offer. "I've never been afraid of anything before," he admitted. "I don't think I let myself be frightened of anything, and this particular fear is irrational. I have the means to continue breathing under-water. If I had died during it, I would have been cloned and a new RH104 introduced. I don't know why that particular incident bothered me so much."

Hannah gave him a look that clearly questioned his intelligence. "Have you considered that this is the first time you've been allowed to explore the human side of yourself? It's normal to be scared of things."

"But the water wouldn't have killed me."

"You can still be scared of it. Humans are sometimes irrational. I'm sorry I pushed you into coming here."

"No!" Rhys's protest was immediate. "I'm glad you did. This isn't like a flooded bulkhead at all."

"And I would miss you if you died," Hannah said.

"I could be cloned. I would come back."

"I'm not sure if you would be the same. You wouldn't have your memories. You wouldn't remember me. You'd be starting over from scratch again."

He'd been afraid of drowning in the bulkhead and having to be regenerated, Rhys realized. He hadn't wanted to die. He wanted to keep the body, life, and memories of his current iteration. It was important that he continued to move forward for her. He hadn't known that until now. "You're correct. I want to keep everything going as it is. I don't want to die again."

"You need to stay alive," Hannah said. "We have a lot of living to do."

He liked how she said "we." He tried to convey that in the look he sent her way. A blush touched her cheeks, a sight he would never stop enjoying.

Did he really look at her like she was the center of the universe? How had he done that? How had her friends noticed?

"Let's go behind the falls," Hannah suggested once their meal was done. "Do you think you'd be okay with that? There's lots of room behind it."

Rhys's vision honed in on the curtain of water flowing into the pool. The falls crested over a cliff shelf. A hollow space about three meters high was hidden behind it. He nodded. "I'd like that."

———

HANNAH HAD PICTURED A MORE romantic scene behind her favorite waterfall—Rhys taking her into his arms, kissing her, pulling at her clothes the way her hands itched to pluck at his perfectly fitting uniform. To her consternation, he stared straight ahead at the sheet of water cascading in front of them. It lightly misted the air, tiny droplets clinging to them.

Disappointment and hurt welled in her at his lack of reaction, but she didn't show it. "Is everything okay? Is this bothering you?"

"No."

"I can tell *something's* wrong." She reached for his hand. To her relief, he curled his around her fingers.

"It's the same as it was last night." Her pulse picked up at the memory. "I still don't know what I'm doing."

She exhaled a shaky sigh of relief. "We've been over that. You're a quick learner. Don't sweat it."

"I had no idea other cyborgs had already started relationships with New Edeners." With his free hand, he pinched the bridge of his nose in frustration. "This is something I should have anticipated happening."

"How? It's not like your people socialized with others that much."

Rhys considered his next words, and a moment passed before he spoke. "That's not entirely accurate. Our ship occasionally made supply runs at stations staffed with people. It wasn't widely discussed, but I know at least a few had physical relations with residents. Those details weren't shared with me."

"Seriously? You aren't a bunch of virgin cyborgs waiting to get jumped?" She couldn't believe what she was hearing. "What about your shared telepathy link?"

"We can't read each other's thoughts. We can communicate with one another, that's all." Rhys's gaze remained trained on the water.

"And what, you think I'd be upset about that? I'm not." She squeezed his hand and was reassured when he returned the gesture. "I'm not going to push you into anything you don't want. It's up to you."

He was quiet again, motionless, except for his thumb stroking the back of her hand. Hannah leaned against him, solid and immovable as a tree, as they stared at the water falling.

"I want it all," he finally said, voice quiet. "I want you more than I've wanted anything."

Hannah shifted so she could better see his face. Her knees went a little weak. The look he sent her—so full of promise and desire—scorched something in her, and she nearly threw herself into his arms. But she remained where she was, wanting him to be in charge of this.

He raised his free hand and brushed aside a few strands of hair that had escaped her braid, then brushed the backs of his fingers against her skin. Hannah's breathing stilled for a couple of seconds as the light touch set every nerve ending in her body aflame. Goosebumps popped up along her skin.

His kiss was gentle, almost hesitant, as if he was nervous she wouldn't like it. Hannah kissed him back, putting everything she could into it. Her arms twined around his neck, pulling him closer. His hands rested on her hips, and he pushed his body against hers, the outline of his erection pressing against her belly. A thrill coursed through her at the sensation. She gently took his lower lip between her teeth and sucked at the tender flesh in a pale imitation of what she'd done to him the night before. His breath stuttered and muscles seized under her touch for half a second, as if he couldn't decide what to do next. Hannah paused in anticipation, waiting for him to make the next move.

He surprised her when he picked her up, sweeping her off the ground as easily as a feather. Her legs instinctively wrapped around his waist, so she was at eye level with him. He looked astonished, eyes wide, but she couldn't tell if it was directed at himself or her. The astonishment gave way to desire, his lips parting a little, as if trying to decide what to do or say next. Hannah lightly kissed him, which he eagerly returned, his tongue demanding entrance to her mouth. She was only too happy to give it.

"What happens next?" she asked against his lips. "What do you want?"

"You brought me here for a reason," he said roughly.

She smiled. "Of course, I had an ulterior motive."

"It's private, it's quiet." He looked away at the water for a moment, indecision warring on his face. "How deep is the water?"

"Less than two meters at the deepest point." She lightly nipped at the pulse point under his ear.

He sucked in a harsh breath and tightened his hold on her ass. "Let's get in."

Hannah didn't need any more encouragement. As soon as he released her, she bolted for the pool, shedding clothes as she did so. She walked into the water, its temperature warmer than she remembered. Maybe it was because she'd gone so long without hot water.

Rhys followed, his eyes never leaving her as she half-paddled through the water. She dunked her head underneath the surface. When she came back up a second later, the desire in his expression had been replaced by concern. She remembered his fear of water. "It's okay," she said. "I can swim and the water isn't deep, anyway." Her feet found the sandy bottom, and she stood up, water gently lapping at her breasts. "See?"

That was all the encouragement he needed. Rhys stripped off his clothes faster than she thought possible. He was already hard, a sight she hadn't forgotten from the night before. She could hardly wait to feel his skin against hers again. A smile of anticipation spread across her face. "What is it?" he asked.

"I'm just thinking that you can get out of a skintight spacesuit a hell of a lot faster than I thought you could."

He strode along the tiny strip of beach and gingerly stepped into the water. He visibly relaxed as its temperature registered, and he took a few experimental steps across the pebbled bottom. "I have a lot of incentive."

Both of them remained rooted to the spot, the only sound the gentle fall of water. Finally, Rhys reached for her wet braid, winding it around his fingers. He let it go and pulled her in for a kiss. It was eager, more confident than she expected after his confession behind the waterfall.

Hannah was only too eager to melt into him, to have him touch her. When his tongue touched her lips, demanding entrance, a moan escaped her, and the sound only encouraged him. His hands drifted down her back to her ass, experimentally kneading the flesh there before gripping her hips again. His cock pressed into her belly, a promise of what she hoped was to come next. Her pulse throbbed between her legs, steady as a drumbeat. If it hadn't been for the water's support and his hold on her, she might have lost her balance.

He lightly nipped at her lower lip, sending a shudder of pleasure through her. "Thank you for bringing me here," he said against her mouth. "I can see why you like this place so much."

"It's private," she said.

"Mm-hmm." His murmur of agreement sent a pleasant vibration through her chest where their skin met. Just as quickly, he moved away, leaving her chilled where they no longer touched. Indecision warred on his face for a second before he crouched, ducking his head underwater.

"Rhys? What the hell?" Hannah didn't move. She watched as he swam a little, not coming up for air. His belly went low to the pebbles at the pool's bottom as he slid along it. "What are you doing?"

He returned to the surface, shaking water off his cropped dark hair. "Just experimenting. I wanted to see if I hate this water as much as the flooded bulkheads." Catching Hannah's quizzical look, he said, "I don't. I don't enjoy having my head underwater, but I can tolerate it when it's warm and clear."

"It's good to know that we might be able to make swimming together a regular part of our activities."

Something shifted in his expression at the word "together," a flash of his metallic eyes that looked remarkably human. "It's you too," he said. "I enjoy spending time with you."

"Not just because I like to get naked with you?" she teased.

That remark actually brought a smile to his face, as if he understood what she was trying to do. "I like that too." He reached for her hand underwater, twining his fingers through hers. "I like everything about you."

This time, his kiss was more sure, more confident. Hannah twined her arms around his neck, the tips of her breasts scraping against his chest, the sensation causing sparks to trail along her skin. But Rhys surprised her when he pulled away. "I want to try something," he said.

Hannah cocked her head to the side, waiting. A thrum of anticipation coursed through her. He hadn't suggested anything like that yet.

"I can breathe underwater," he said.

She nodded.

"What you did for me," he continued slowly. "I'd like to . . ."

Understanding dawned, bright and hot as a flame. "Oh, hell, yes." Rhys started to crouch, but she put a hand on his shoulder, stopping him. "If the water bothers you, stop," she said. "I won't mind."

He nodded and ducked his head underneath.

Hannah's hands reached for his hair, stroking the short strands as his mouth gently kissed her belly. The feeling of it and the warm water around her—alien, strange, and thrilling—drew a mewl from her throat and he'd hardly started. He reached for her leg, draping her knee over his shoulder as he knelt on the pebbles. He put one hand where her hip met her ass to steady her and the other on her upper thigh, dangerously close to where she wanted it the most.

His tongue traced along her sensitive skin, a tease that was almost unbearable. Her muscles shook, insides already coiling themselves in excitement at what was in store for her. "Rhys," she said, voice rough. She hoped he could hear her. "I want . . ."

His hold grew a little tighter and he gasped against her skin. For a second, she thought he might have to tap out, that being underwater was too much for him, but his mouth found the spot already begging for his attention.

She cried out, fingers grasping his hair and her legs shaking against him. "Oh, my God!"

His tongue slid along her core, setting its nerves alight and her body almost rigid. She knew she wouldn't last long, that she was going to fall apart against his face if he kept doing that. She desperately hoped he wouldn't stop.

He slid one finger inside her, drawing another cry from her throat. "Like that," she panted. Her lingering thoughts about whether he could hear her were answered as he slipped another finger into her as his mouth worked her clit. The leg she still stood on buckled in pleasure and she slipped, falling backward in the water.

Rhys stood up like a shot, pulling her back upright. His eyes were glazed over, half-hooded with lust, and she knew she looked the same. His hand slid down her belly, back to her pussy, his fingers sliding inside her. "I wanted to watch," he murmured.

Hannah's body arched against his hand as her orgasm ripped through her, coaxing a yell from her that might've been heard from outer space. She didn't care as she rode his hand, Rhys's eyes never leaving hers as her climax crested over again. It wasn't until she leaned back in the water, shaking and sated, that he pulled his fingers out of her.

Their gazes caught and held. Hannah let herself float on her back, content to let the water hold her for a moment as she recovered. Rhys watched her, a hungry look on his face. "That was amazing," she said. "I wasn't expecting that." She let out a shaky laugh.

Rhys grabbed her and hauled her against him. His cock jutted against her, a reminder that he still hadn't found his satisfaction, and he reached under the water, quickly stroking it like he was trying to placate it. She bit back a smile and wrapped her own hand around it, sliding it up and down the sensitive flesh. Now it was his turn to moan, and his eyes drifted shut for a few seconds. His hips pumped against her hand in a pale imitation of what he truly wanted. She wanted that too.

"Come on," she said. She grabbed his hand and led him out of the water to the blanket they'd used for their meal, sitting down. He did the same, then reached for her face, trailing his fingers along her jaw. She closed her eyes as sparks danced along her skin where he touched it. Goosebumps popped up along her flesh, but whether it was from evaporating water or in anticipation—or both— she couldn't say. A small, rational voice in the back of her mind told her she should've brought towels.

"What are you thinking about?" Rhys asked.

"I'm a little cold," she admitted.

In a flash, she was flat on her back, Rhys kneeling over her. His hands bracketed either side of her head, his knees on either side of hers. A thrill coursed through her, and she couldn't keep a smile from her face. Rhys's expression was shocked, like he couldn't believe he had just done that. "Smooth," she murmured.

"I'm sorry?" He looked like he was going to move away, but she put a proprietary hand on his shoulder to keep him where he was.

"That was smooth," she said. "Feel free to do that any time."

He hesitated. "I don't know why I did that."

"You're following your instincts. Your *human* instincts." Hannah tilted her face up to kiss him, which he eagerly returned. His cock bobbed against her belly, an unbearable tease. "I'm into it."

He urged her knees apart with one of his own. Her hips bucked involuntarily against his body, wanting more. Her breath caught and her pulse sped up, ticking along in anticipation of what was about to happen. Indecision warred with lust in his expression for a few seconds, and his metallic gaze caught hers. They stared at each other for a moment. She was certain he could hear her heart beating a rapid tattoo.

She was right. "I've never seen your vital signs like this," he murmured.

She bit the inside of her cheek to keep from giggling. "I don't think they've ever been measured," she replied. Her hips lifted again, encouraging him, and she hooked a leg around his.

"I don't want to hurt you."

"You won't. I'd tell you if you did, anyway."

"Do you promise?"

She nodded.

He reached between their bodies for his shaft, and Hannah did the same, guiding him. He pushed inside her, drawing a sharp moan from her. The motion was more gentle than she expected, a tease that was driving her out of her mind. His face was a mask of concentration as he fought for control, something she wished he would give up. She stroked his face, thumb gliding over his lips. He bit it, the small pain an unexpected pleasure as he drove himself home, their bodies meeting.

The sensation was so intense, both of them cried out. Rhys was still, eyes locked on hers in surprise. It quickly gave way to lust, and his body trembled above and inside hers. She felt full and a strange but welcome sense of completion, like this was right and supposed to happen.

"Hannah," he murmured through gritted teeth. "I . . ."

"Do it," she urged him. She rolled her hips against him in encouragement, the motion drawing a shudder of pleasure from him. She tightened her leg around his.

"I don't . . ." His words died as he thrust inside her.

Any retort Hannah might have offered evaporated at the sensation.

As he did it again, all rational thought ceased. Everything around them may as well have not existed as he drove into her. What he lacked in experience, he made up for in enthusiasm. Not that Hannah cared.

His breaths became more labored, came faster, and she knew he was close. She tightened her hold on him, nails digging into his back as his tempo increased. She hadn't expected to climax again, but the angle at which his body struck hers . . . She felt the familiar ripples of pleasure course through her and she let them explode, biting into his shoulder to muffle her wail.

She could hardly control her own reflexes as she came down. Rhys was still on his way, and with her last vestiges of strength, she urged her hips to match his rhythm.

It worked. He shuddered above and inside her as he came, a twisted look of pure bliss on his face. She'd never seen that before. She wanted to see it again.

Both of them were quiet for a few moments, the only sounds their breathing and the waterfall a few meters away. Rhys leaned over and kissed her before pulling out of her body and lying on the blanket next to her.

Hannah rolled on her side to face him, propping herself up on one elbow. "That was fun."

He nodded. "I think I understand what I was missing before." He kissed her again, then lay back against the wrinkled picnic blanket. Hannah tucked her head on his shoulder, and he wrapped an arm around her.

For the first time in years, she was happy.

For the first time in her life, she thought she might be in love.

CHAPTER ELEVEN

THEY TOOK another swim after they had sex, then lay twined together on the blanket for what felt like hours. Rhys's internal chronometer reminded him that it was only twenty minutes. Every one of his senses and sensors was trained on her. The feel of her weight against his body, her skin on his. The smell of her hair, fragranced with the clean smell of the water they'd played in. If he'd been capable of it, he would have blushed at the memory.

The twin suns were beginning to set when they started for home. This time, Rhys was the one to take Hannah's hand, not wanting to let her go. It was a curious feeling, one he welcomed, and he scoured the depths of his original's and incarnations' memory shards as they strode along the dirt road. Had they ever felt like he did now? He had the vague notion that the original Rhys Hammond slept around quite a bit, had never settled down nor wanted to, and wondered where his ability to fixate on one woman had come from.

But fixate, he did. He never wanted to be apart from her again. He could hardly wait until they returned home and he could see what it was like having sex with her in a real bed.

"What are you thinking?" Hannah asked, squeezing his hand.

"That I'd like to try that again, as soon as possible."

She turned scandalized eyes to him, the color in her cheeks high. "Me too."

"I didn't know what I was missing until now. I'm glad I could share that with you."

"You said before that your crew would sometimes go off your ship to meet others," she said, voice a little halting. "You never told me why you didn't do the same."

"I preferred the ship." The ship had meant safety and familiarity, long denied to his previous iterations.

"Can I ask you a weird question?"

"Of course. You can ask me anything," he replied.

"Did any old memories return from the first Rhys?" A pensive look he couldn't read crossed her features, as if she was afraid of the answer.

"Back at the waterfall? No, that was all me." He stopped in his tracks. Hannah did likewise. He tucked a damp lock of hair behind her ear and thought she'd never looked more beautiful as she did now, in the deepening twilight. "I'd rather make memories with you on New Eden." He hoped his words didn't sound too mechanical, that he'd finally mastered a more human style.

A genuine smile bloomed on her face, and he knew he'd said the right thing. "I'm really glad to hear that."

They continued on their walk, the pleasant feel of her hand in his a balm to his soul he hadn't known he needed. His sensors picked up her calm and steady heartbeat, and in that instant, he wished her body could do the same. That she could know at an instinctual level that he was content. *I'm happy*, he thought. *For the first time in my life.*

"I'm glad to hear that too," she said.

He stopped again. "What? How?" Alarm threaded through him. Had what they shared at the waterfall resulted in the same kind of broadcast connection like the one he shared with his brethren? Had . . .

"You just said it out loud," Hannah replied, as if he was insane.

"I did?" Quickly, Rhys brought up his brain's central processing unit's reports to verify her claim. He had, indeed, said the words aloud. "Huh."

"Is something wrong?"

"No, I don't think so. I believe I just had a very human response for the first time since I've been in this iteration."

She lightly poked him in the ribs, drawing a smile from him. Who would've guessed he was ticklish? "I think what happened back there also counts as a very human response."

"I meant that I've never said aloud what I was thinking. I believe it's more common among strictly organic beings." His body tightened when he thought of the waterfall, his processor replaying images of Hannah in the water, his face between her thighs, then her body beneath his. He bit back a groan.

"Enjoy being human, then," Hannah said. "It can get messy, but it's a lot of fun."

That she could say such things when she'd grown up in an increasingly decaying colony floored him. She had a flinty exterior that Rhys and the other cyborgs admired—Hannah Forsyth could get things done in a way none of them had expected from an organic human who had so little to work with—but there was optimism beneath her hardness. She truly believed that New Eden could improve, that Rhys and his brethren could thrive with them. He was honored that she wanted them to stay, that she had given herself to him. That she liked him as much as he did her.

He'd never experienced this kind of affection for another person. He liked it.

"I'd still like it if you could take me off-world sometime," she continued. "New Eden's always going to be home, but I want to see the rest of the galaxy."

"It's enormous."

"Yeah, I know. But what about just beyond New Eden?"

"Your planet is very isolated. The closest point to inhabited space is the waystation I told you about that's a two-to-three-day voyage away at our ship's top speeds, which is faster than most other vessels. Your ancestors certainly chose a very isolated place to settle."

"No shit." The words were tinged with bitterness. "At least we'll be able to communicate with other people soon enough, won't we?"

Work had yet to begin on the communication center's reconstruction, although Rhys had every faith it would be an efficient job. "Yes. You also have my word that I will take you off-planet sooner rather than later."

"I just want to see what's out there," she said softly. As if to emphasize her point, she looked up at the twilight sky. A few stars had already appeared.

"Not all of it is good," Rhys said. "At least the bad parts are far enough away that you won't have to worry about them."

"Do I want to know?" Just as quickly, she answered herself. "Tell me. Would New Eden have to fortify itself?"

"I don't think this planet has the resources that anyone with nefarious intentions would want, not to mention its isolation. This entire sector of the galaxy is largely ignored, anyway. Each planet and station operates individually, without a central government."

"Are there places with them in place?"

"Elsewhere in the galaxy, none this remote. It's simply too large and sparsely populated."

As he said the words, a memory shard resurfaced—Rhys kneeling on the ground, hands bound behind him. The shadow of a black-suited male loomed over him, face hidden by a helmet. Rhys could see his own face in its reflective visor, revealing the image of a man who tried to remain stoic in the face of certain death, but whose lips twitched in barely suppressed terror. Distantly, he was aware of Hannah's calling to him out of concern, but he couldn't bring himself to pull away from the scenario replaying in his mind's eye.

He was watching himself die, again. Something about it said he wasn't observing the demise of his clones as he had before, but the original Rhys Hammond.

His breath hitched, and his internal sensors sounded alarms about an impending systems shutdown. He ignored them, forcing the memory to unfold.

It was as if he was trying to watch the scene underwater. Colors shifted and rippled and the sounds were distorted. It was difficult to focus on what he was seeing, but he waited, breath paused in anticipation.

"A coup," the mysterious man in black said. "Hammond, what you're describing is a coup."

"We did not sign up for this program to be tortured," Rhys heard himself say. Despite the abject terror that left a hard lump in his throat, his original's voice was strangely calm. Rhys had the sense that his original had come to terms with his death and just wanted it to be over. The anticipation was the worst part.

"You signed up to do what you were told to do," the man in black snapped.

"I was not brought on to this project for these reasons," Rhys protested. "What you're doing is inhumane. None of these people signed up for this." His fright ebbed away as his voice rose in anger. "This was *not* the original aim of the project. It . . ."

The man in black stripped off one of his gloves, revealing the same ports and bare electrodes embedded in the skin that Rhys had. He placed his bare hand on Rhys's shoulder and squeezed. Electricity arced through him, his sensors flashing warnings about an impending full systems organic and cybernetic failure.

Everything went dark. The ground gave way beneath his feet, and he collapsed to the ground, scrubby grass and dirt meeting him as his body fell.

"Rhys!"

It took a few seconds for his systems to come back online and his lungs to resume breathing, even longer for his ears to register that it was Hannah screaming. He flexed his hands, then rolled over, half-aided by Hannah, whose tear-streaked face greeted him. "What just happened?" she sobbed.

He fumbled with his words. "I'm not . . I had a flashback."

"You've never had one like that before! You were out of it for way too long! You passed out!" She hauled him into a sitting position. "What the hell kind of flashback was that?"

"I saw myself die." Just saying the words made Rhys's throat clog with emotion, like he had witnessed the death of a beloved family member instead of his original. In a way, he supposed his original *was* a family member, one who hadn't had anyone to mourn him since his murder.

Her face softened. "Not again."

"It wasn't a clone," he continued, steeling himself. "It was the original Rhys's death. I've never remembered that before. He was murdered."

"Weren't some of your previous clones murdered? What a horrible thing to keep experiencing over and over." She wiped her eyes with the back of her hand.

"This was different. The original Rhys had much more agency than my clones did. He did something that his superiors didn't like." When he was sure he could do so without falling over, he stood up. Hannah helped him, not that he needed it, but he held on to her all the same. It felt good to touch her. It was even better that she cared about him.

"He led a coup," Rhys said. He dusted himself off. "Or tried to. I don't know if it was successful."

Hannah's eyes widened. "Maybe that's why all of you are just cruising through space alone. You escaped something."

Of course, they had. Rhys had suspected as much, even though it was never discussed among his brethren. "We don't know what we ran away from."

"It must have been successful. One of your clones must've managed to break free from whoever was holding on to you. There must be a way to remember that somehow. Maybe on your ship?"

That was doubtful. Rhys and the others could become a part of the ship when they wanted to. They would have been aware of every sensor, every computer command and encrypted byte in the vessel's memory banks. Whatever had led them to wandering around deep space on the farthest edges of the galaxy wouldn't be found on their ship.

But Rhys couldn't keep having these flashbacks. They

were getting more intense, the reactions more physical. He had no idea how his cybernetics would continue to handle them, nor how he could make them stop.

"Perhaps," he said, knowing she was expecting an answer. He would have to consult his fellow cyborgs. As far as he knew, none of them had experienced what he had. He changed the subject, wanting to put her mind at ease. "Let's go home. We'll discuss this later."

She looked doubtful. "Are you sure?"

"I don't want to remain on the path all night, do you?" His newfound fears about his past notwithstanding, the memories of what they'd shared at the waterfall persisted, along with his need to do it again. He hoped he put the right amount of suggestion into his voice. "There are other things I'd rather be doing, besides."

She blushed, a reaction he would never tire of seeing or being the cause of. It was one of his favorite of her organic features. Her next words were more serious than he would have liked. "Are you sure? You just passed out. Has that even happened before?"

"No," he replied truthfully.

"Rhys . . ."

"I will talk about it with the other cyborgs," he said. "They may have insight about what happened to me. I promise I'll talk about this with them tomorrow, before we start work on the communication tower and launchpad."

She didn't look convinced. "Promise?"

"When have I ever been untruthful with you?"

"Good point. Can cyborgs lie?"

He hadn't expected that question. "I don't know. I never have."

She nodded, seemingly satisfied with his answer. "How do you feel now?"

"Steady and back to full capacity." At least he felt so

physically. Emotionally, mentally, he was still shaken by what he had just experienced.

Hannah clasped her hand around his. He gently squeezed it, grateful for the connection. "Let's go home."

———

A FEW HOURS LATER, while Hannah slept sprawled across him, Rhys lay awake in bed, listening to her deep, steady breathing. His enhanced brain, ever efficient, had neatly compartmentalized the feel of her against him and replayed what they'd shared when they returned to the house, while another part mulled over his increasingly worrying flashbacks.

He needed the advice of the other cyborgs. As much as he was loath to possibly disturb others, there were some issues only cyborgs could examine and pull apart. For the first time in what felt like forever, he uploaded himself to their shared broadcast network, all but abandoned since they landed on New Eden. He sent out a greeting, wanting to know if anyone else in the immediate area was still awake at half past three in the morning.

To his surprise, SP29 was. *Let's walk*, the other cyborg suggested. *I need to get out of this house.*

Rhys was surprised to hear that, given SP29's hostess was Hannah's best friend and had been nothing but hospitable since they arrived. *I'll be outside in a moment*, he replied.

He delicately unwound Hannah from him. She stirred a little but didn't wake, and his sensors told him she was still deeply asleep when Rhys tucked the frayed bedsheet around her a little more snugly. At the last second, he leaned over to kiss her cheek. He could've sworn she smiled in her sleep at the gesture. His heart swelled at the sight.

He quickly dressed, then stole through the house to the front door. SP29 waited outside as he closed it behind him as silently as he could.

SP29's gaze traveled along Rhys's face. *Good night?*

Rhys hesitated. How much did he know? It wasn't as if they could read each other's minds in the telepathic sense. But SP29 was his friend. All of the cyborgs were. Might as well be honest. *Yes.*

Guided by the light of the stars and the pair of half moons overhead, they strolled along the dusty path that wound around the houses. Neither of them spoke until they reached the meadow where their ship waited. "So, then, what's wrong?" SP29 finally asked aloud.

"How often do you have flashbacks about your previous clones?"

SP29 shrugged. "Very rarely. I haven't had any since we landed here. I can't say I miss them. Why?"

"When you did, what were they like?"

"I told everyone when I had them, same as the rest. They were always short, maybe three or four seconds, usually something mundane. Why? Are they bothering you?"

An uncharacteristic nervousness twisted something in Rhys, and it took a few seconds for the words to come. "I have them a lot," he began.

"You've been cloned more than the rest of us. That makes sense." SP29 kept his vision pinned on the ship, his expression unreadable.

"No, it's worse." Rhys tried again. "Mine are violent. I've seen myself killed. Tonight, I saw my original being murdered."

SP29's gaze snapped back to Rhys. "What?"

"I think my original tried to lead a coup."

SP29 appeared unfazed by that theory. "Well, yeah, somewhere along the line, we rebelled."

"But don't you want to know why?" Rhys pressed. "We've been drifting through deep space and cloning ourselves as we die off for years, and we have no idea why."

"Whatever it was, it was bad," SP29 replied. "We've always agreed that it was best for us to stay in the fringes of space and stick to ourselves. It was instinctual. We've always known it was dangerous for people like us in civilized space."

"People?" Rhys hadn't heard any of them refer to themselves as such.

Irritation crossed SP29's face, something Rhys couldn't remember having seen from him before. "We're people who have some cybernetic enhancements. Cyborgs are people."

Rhys couldn't resist asking, "Why do you still go by your cyborg designation?"

"I don't think my original was the nicest person. I'm not sure I want to be Samuel Pelletier." He shrugged. "I'm still thinking about who and what I am and what I want to be."

"Is there something you want to talk about?"

SP29 looked like was about to speak, then hesitated. "It's complicated."

"How the hell is any of this uncomplicated?"

"Fair point. It's about Jasmine and DL16. Darius," he quickly added.

"I didn't know DL16 chose a new name."

"Why would you? You've been spending a lot of time with Hannah. It hasn't gone unnoticed." Before Rhys could respond to that, SP29 added, "That's what normal people do. It's good that we're forming relationships. I'm not angry."

"You still haven't told me why things are complicated for you."

SP29 exhaled and looked away. "What do you know about love triangles?"

The term was foreign to Rhys. "Nothing."

"Then I'm not sure you'll be able to help me." He changed the subject. "You said you saw your original being killed?"

"He was executed in cold blood. He was on his knees, hands bound behind his back, while someone in our uniform accused him of leading a coup."

"Did you recognize the face or voice?"

"No, it wasn't one of us." A possible explanation struck Rhys. "Do you think there were others like us, and we did away with their DNA after we took back our independence?"

SP29 shrugged.

"Consider it," Rhys urged. "What would have been the point of enhancing and cloning only twenty men? There must have been an army of us at one point."

"What about an army of five or ten each? Why recruit one hundred men for a fucked-up military project when twenty will suffice, then clone each five times?"

SP29's theory made sense. "Damn it."

"We agreed not to look too closely into our past," SP29 reminded him. "We all thought it best to simply move forward and live our lives peacefully. There's no point in looking behind us."

"There is when the flashbacks are causing the physical symptoms mine are," Rhys retorted. Anger tugged at him, an unfamiliar emotion that he already hated. He didn't want to be angry with his friend, who didn't care about the problems he was having nearly as much as he expected. "I passed out on the path today after I saw myself being murdered. I want to know why this is happening, so I can put a stop to it. Don't you?"

"My original was likely a terrible person, as was yours. Kind and sane people don't take part in building up a cybernetic army. We're weapons of war, Rhys." SP29 held up his palms to show off the ports in them, the same ones Rhys had. With a single touch, they could send a lethal rush of energy through an organic being.

"Kind and sane people don't execute others, either," Rhys replied. "Do you want to know what I saw?"

SP29 folded his arms across his chest. "Fine, send it to me."

The memory from his flashback was intact, a file saved in his enhanced brain. Rhys ported the memory to SP29, whose eyes flashed brightly as he absorbed it. "Fuck," he muttered.

"I can't keep living like this," Rhys said. "I have no idea why my brain keeps doing it. Except for a couple of instances, I don't know what's triggering them. They're getting worse."

"And you think knowing the cause of them will make all of this stop, or do you want a surgical intervention?"

"Surgery could erase everything."

"We could clone you again."

"No." Rhys's answer was immediate. "Absolutely not. I don't want to lose Hannah."

SP29 regarded him thoughtfully for a moment, considering the weight of his refusal. "You're understanding what it is to be human now, aren't you?"

"I just don't want to forget her."

SP29 pinched the bridge of his nose between his fingers. "I'll help you figure this out," he said. "Although, if there are any answers to be found on New Eden, they're probably in your head. You're the original cyborg. You've been cloned the most often."

Rhys nodded. "I'll help you out as best I can with your Jasmine and Darius problem."

"I appreciate the offer, but I'm not sure you can."

"Why not?"

"The way you feel about Hannah?" SP29 said. Rhys nodded. "That's how I feel about both of them."

Surprise wouldn't let Rhys reply.

"So, things for me are complicated," SP29 continued. He nodded his head back in the direction of the houses. "Let's go home. We'll work on your problem in the morning." He quickly corrected himself when his chronometer reminded him of the time. "I suppose it's already morning."

"Later in the morning." SP29 finally smiled. "We're people. We don't have to be so pedantic anymore."

CHAPTER TWELVE

Hannah stirred and reached across the bed for Rhys. All she touched was a cold bedsheet. She sat up and looked around the bedroom. "Rhys?" Slipping out from under the covers, she padded along the floor to the landing. "Rhys?" she repeated. A light glowed downstairs.

She found him in the kitchen, seated at the table, nursing a glass of water. He brightened when he saw her. "You're up early."

"I'm always up early." She took the seat across from him. "Is everything all right?"

He gave a half shrug. "I think so, between us, at least." Warmth rose in her at his words. Just as quickly, it was gone when his expression grew serious. "I spoke to SP29 earlier. Neither of us could sleep."

"Through your link?"

"And verbally. We went for a walk." He hesitated. Something twisted in Hannah's stomach at the indecisive look on his face.

"And?" she prompted him.

"Hannah, what I'm about to say to you—it's private. It needs to stay between us."

"Of course." Her discomfort bloomed into full-blown concern, bordering on panic. "Is he okay?"

"No, but he isn't unwell in the ways you might think." He looked away for a few seconds, color suffusing his cheeks. Was he *blushing?*

Her concern gave way to confusion. "Rhys, just tell me what's going on with him. Maybe I can help."

"It's about your friend Jasmine too."

She could have collapsed on the tabletop in relief. "If this is about SP29 having a thing for her, he has nothing to worry about. I assure you, anything he has in mind, she'll be up for it."

"SP29 has feelings for her and DL16. Darius," he corrected himself.

It took a few seconds for Rhys's meaning to sink in. "*Oh,*" Hannah said in surprise.

"I had no idea. I don't know if Darius knows, either. SP29 is struggling with those feelings right now."

"Well, yeah. Holy shit, that must be torture for him."

Rhys's eyes raised in surprise. "You're not upset?"

"Of course not. He is who he is." Now it was Hannah's turn to feel a little awkward at what she'd have to say next. "I don't think Jasmine would mind, to be honest with you."

"That SP29 has feelings for two people?"

"No. I think she'd welcome it." She pinned him with a stare. "Do you see where I'm going with this?"

Rhys was silent for a moment as he considered the implication. When it hit him, it was like an old-fashioned lightbulb flicked on in his mind. "Oh."

"Yeah."

"You won't tell Jasmine about this, will you? It's very important to SP29 that he handles this in his own time."

"Of course I won't say anything, as long as you don't tell anyone that Jasmine would totally be willing to have two boyfriends who are into her and each other." She leaned back in her seat, the old wood squeaking in protest. "Wow, this is our first secret between us."

"Is it common for couples to keep secrets about their friends?"

"Yeah, I think so." She yawned. "Come back to bed for another couple of hours. We both need sleep." Rhys opened his mouth, as if to protest, but she cut him off before he could speak. "Your computer bits need down-time as much as your organics do. Plus, I sleep better with you in the bed. Let's go."

Rhys drained his glass and left it in the sink. Wrapping an arm around her waist, he nipped at her earlobe, drawing a squeak from her. A frisson of heat ribboned through her despite her exhaustion. "Let's go back to bed."

———

THE LANDING PAD'S repair was the day's priority and necessary if they were going to bring in supplies from off-world. Hannah led Rhys on a tour through the ruined facility, pointing out the comms board where she'd sent that fateful SOS months ago. He picked up the yellowed book of instructions and distress codes, leafing through the crumbling pages. "It was a lot of touching wires together to see what would spark," Hannah said. She pointed at a comms board that had to be hundreds of years old. An ancient keyboard with buttons had been attached to it, the letters on the keys long worn away. "That thing hardly worked at all. I had to guess which key was which letter."

"We received your verbal SOS," Rhys explained.

"Oh, so I spent all those hours trying to type for nothing." There was a levity in her voice, despite her words.

"Unfortunate, yet not a waste of time. Your message was sent on an old Omega Three channel, which is why no one but us picked it up. The tech is too old for modern spacecraft to recognize."

"And yours did." Hannah ran her fingers over the keyboard, sending dust particles into the air.

Rhys picked up a loose comm array and turned it over to inspect it. Its bottom panel had rotted or been torn away, revealing loose bundles of wires. No water damage, though, so some of the components might be salvageable. "Our ship is equipped to recognize transmissions on all known channels."

"Why?"

He nearly replied with his own question as to why their ship could do that but paused. The conversation with SP29 lingered in his mind, especially their questions about their existence. Did they retain all that old tech in case whoever started the cyborg project came after them? What were the odds, after their being alone in space for so many years? "I don't know," he slowly replied. He turned around the room, taking in the broken tables and tech, the dirt and debris littering the floor. "SP29 and I talked about that last night too." He kept his voice low, not wanting the other cyborgs inspecting the facility to hear them.

"About why you keep century-old tech aboard your ship?"

"In part. We don't know why we exist, Hannah." Was he malfunctioning, or did his voice catch?

She looked at him a little sadly. "I guess you have time to think about that now."

"We always did, we just . . . didn't bother to. I'm not sure if I like contemplating my reasons for existing over and over. All I know is that I wasn't a particularly good person before now."

"Of course you are. You came here to help us."

"No, I mean the original Rhys Hammond. I don't know how to explain it, but he wasn't good. He agreed with whatever the original cyborg program was, agreed with its reasons for existing, and then something happened that made him change his mind." He remembered the shadow looming over him, the horrific knowledge that he was about to die for the first time. "I think I'd like to find out why we exist."

A shadow crossed over her face. "Are you sure?"

He nodded. "I need to know my origins. I don't know if the others would agree with me, nor do I know how to start searching, but I think I'd like to find out the reasons for myself."

"I get that." She picked up a coupler that she'd clumsily soldered together. "Maybe knowing that would help with the flashbacks."

It might give some context to them. Rhys held out his hand for the coupler, and she obediently placed it in his palm. "Did you repair this?" he asked, changing the subject. A piece of it was melted in place.

"As best as I could. It involved a lot of fire, and I had to sacrifice a spoon from my ancestors' old world set to melt the metal." She sighed.

"I'm sorry you lost your cutlery."

"It was worth it." She smiled at him, a ray of sunshine in the darkened room. "So, how bad is it?"

"We have pieces aboard the ship that we can use to bring communications back online. I'll have to speak to the others about the state of the landing pad itself."

SP29 strode into the room. "I heard that. The pad's in rough shape. It has to be completely rebuilt, and the materials will have to come from off-world. There's nothing on New Eden that can be used. Hannah, do you know where the original colonists sourced their building materials?"

"As far as I know, they brought everything they needed with them from the old world."

"Makes sense. It will be faster to make a supply run to a waystation for supplies." SP29 cast a critical eye over the comms room. "Would you be put out if we just razed everything and rebuilt it from the ground up?"

"Not if it will be the fastest and easiest way to get everything online." Giddiness flowed through Hannah as she said the words. It was finally happening. New Eden was being rebuilt, better and stronger than before. "How long do you think the construction would take?"

SP29 shrugged. "Including the supply run and the demolition of the original site? A month, maybe."

"Oh, my God!" Rhys had said as much, but to have it confirmed so casually felt like a miracle. Like the power station coming back online, Hannah could hardly believe how quickly things happened now. She wondered if she would ever get used to it. She blinked away tears of relief, but not before Rhys noticed them.

"Hannah, are you all right?"

She took a watery breath. "Yes. Don't mind me."

"I'd like to get an inventory going for our first supply run," SP29 continued. "I think the current priorities are supplies for a hospital and a comms tower."

The mention of a hospital gave Hannah pause, and she felt like an idiot for not considering that sooner. "We don't have a doctor."

"Two of our cyborgs are medics," Rhys said. "They're living in communal quarters on the west side of the settlement."

"There may be off-worlders who want to relocate here," SP29 pointed out.

Once again, Hannah felt foolish for not having considered that. "Would people really want to move to New Eden?" she asked incredulously.

"Of course. This is a quiet community, surrounded by nature. There are plenty of people who would like to join this type of settlement, including medical personnel."

"Wow." She couldn't imagine wanting to leave anywhere in civilized space for a backwater planet like New Eden. She hoped she wasn't the one in charge by the time they'd opened immigration to off-worlders. Maybe Rodelle would be up to the task when that came about. Or one of the cyborgs. "Rhys, do you think . . ." The words died in her throat when she faced him. His pallor had changed, like he was about to be sick. His eyes were glassy. "Are you having a flashback?"

He swayed on his feet. She and SP29 rushed to him before he could collapse to the floor. "Fuck!" she yelped. He was dead weight against her, nearly causing her to lose her footing. SP29 nudged her out of the way, then helped Rhys to the floor. "This happened last night too," she said, voice catching.

They knelt beside him. Rhys's eyes stared into nothing, then closed. The motion reminded Hannah of a baby doll she'd played with as a child, with its creepy blinking eyes. "Rhys!" she shouted. "Wake up!" To SP29, she said, "It wasn't like this before!"

Rhys's breathing slowed. With it, Hannah thought her heart also might be stopping. After a horrifying moment, his chest started to rise and fall again, albeit far too slowly.

SP29 paled. "He's gone into shutdown."

"What do you mean?"

"It's like a coma." The other cyborg's voice was

strained. Hannah's heart thudded against her ribs as she waited for him to continue. "This is what happens when a cyborg's lifespan is ending. It's time for him to be cloned again."

Hannah finally tore her gaze from Rhys's expressionless face. She thought she might be sick. "No."

"I don't know why this happened now, but . . ."

"No! Find one of your medical cyborgs and fix this!"

"I don't know if that can be done."

"Try!" she screamed. SP29 flinched. "I know he doesn't want to be cloned again. I know he wants to stay in this body." Iteration, he'd called himself. "There must be something you can try!" When SP29 didn't stand up, she did. "Tell me who the medics are. Now." Through her tears, she hoped she injected enough authority into her voice to get her point across.

SP29 finally got to his feet. "You're right. I know he didn't want that." His expression grew pensive, and she knew he was speaking to the others through their link. After what felt like hours, he announced, "They're on their way."

"What will happen if they can't save him?"

SP29 hesitated, and she had her answer. They would clone him again, grow a new Rhys, but he wouldn't be the man she loved. Would a new version of him even remember her? Rhys only recalled horrible memories, nothing good from his previous lives.

Boots thundered on the floor as their fellow cyborgs ran toward the comms room. The only sound was their footsteps as they shuffled around, picking up Rhys and carrying him away, his body stiff as a board. She guessed they were speaking through their shared broadcast link. "Where are you taking him?" She didn't try to keep the panic out of her voice.

"The ship," SP29 replied. "Everything we need to help him is there."

They meant the cloning tech. She had to make sure they wouldn't try cloning him before exhausting all other options. "I'm going with you."

He looked like he wanted to argue. There must have been something on Hannah's face that brooked no argument, because he merely nodded.

She had to jog to keep up with him as they marched away from the landing pad. Heat blazed from the twin suns, their light nearly blinding her, but she didn't care. All she could focus on was his body, carried by a pair of stony-faced cyborgs.

Their ship waited in the field, dark and hulking in the sunlight. At the cyborgs' approach, its exterior door opened and the ramp extended. Her vision blurred as they carried Rhys up the ramp, and she realized she was crying. She raced after them, footsteps pounding along the black metallic ramp. SP29 grabbed her shoulder, stopping her. She hadn't realized he was behind her. "Don't," he said.

"Fuck you!"

The cyborg's eyes widened in shock, but he didn't reply.

Any guilt Hannah might have felt at her response evaporated when she thought of Rhys aboard that ship. "I'm going after him," she said. She impatiently brushed away tears with her hand. "I've lost almost everyone I've ever loved on this fucking planet. I'm not going to lose him too." And if she had to, she wanted to be there in his final moments.

"We can bring him back," SP29 said, but his protest was weak. He'd been on New Eden long enough to recognize that each clone was different. SP30 wouldn't be a new version of his twenty-ninth self, and it was no different for Rhys.

Hannah shook her head. "You can't. I'm here for Rhys, not for another clone. You aren't interchangeable!" She felt like shaking him to get her point across, for all the good someone her size could do to a solid muscle and metal man.

Everyone else had already disappeared into the belly of the ship. The ramp remained extended, the darkness inside an invitation. "It's going to be bad in there," SP29 warned her. "Have you ever seen surgery?"

"I've seen livestock give birth."

"This won't be like that." He looked at the doorway, expression desolate. "You're right about all this. He wouldn't be the same person if he was cloned again, and I think he would want you there." His voice wavered. "Let's go."

It took a moment for Hannah's vision to adjust to the ship's darkness. She stumbled through the airlock, trying to remember the craft's layout from her tour with Rhys. In retrospect, he hadn't shown her that much, only the recharging pods and a storage closet. Where would a sickbay be? How fast had those cyborgs moved, anyway?

As though he could read her mind, SP29 took her elbow. "Follow me."

She didn't argue, just sniffled and did as he told her. "What will they do?" she asked as they strode through the corridors. A low grinding noise sounded, and an odd odor filled the air, probably due to the ship coming online.

"When a cyborg is in the catatonic state Rhys is in, our usual protocol is to extract his tech and DNA, then start the cloning process again."

"They aren't going to do that today, are they?" Hannah wailed.

"No." SP29's voice was firm.

"How do you know?"

He tapped the side of his head. "We're changing our protocols about these events."

That provided a small measure of relief. "What if they can't fix him?"

"Then we'll begin the cloning procedure. Rhys has been cloned a number of times. He'll always come back."

The words were enough to momentarily halt Hannah in her tracks. "No, he won't. He wouldn't be Rhys, he would be RH104, and you know it!"

"He would have the same basic personality components. He would . . ."

"He would be an entirely different person! Isn't this what we've been debating since you came here? You're all different people with some matching DNA!" She scrubbed a hand over her face. "Look, I don't want to fight with you about this right now. Take me to the sickbay. I need to see Rhys."

In the corridor's dim lighting, she saw a line worry itself between his eyebrows. She wondered what he was thinking, what their hive mind was telling him. "All right."

They were silent, save for Hannah's soft sobs, until they reached the sickbay, or what passed for a sickbay. It didn't look like any medical facility she had dreamed of, or even New Eden's single, dilapidated clinic, with its two hospital beds, the structure now in pieces. There were more recharging pods in the sickbay, but these were on the floor, like a traditional bed, and had more wires and tech lining them. A giant clear tank rested in the middle of the room, filled with water. Round metal balls floated in it. What was a pool doing in the sickbay?

She answered herself just as quickly. That had to be where clones were grown. A shudder rippled down her spine.

She dragged her vision away from the tank to the man

held in place in one of the pods. His clothing had been stripped away, and a group of cyborgs had gathered around him, working in silence. One of them looked up at the ceiling as a panel in it opened. A wicked-looking blade dropped down with a barely audible hiss, directly over Rhys's head.

"They're going to cut him open," Hannah whispered to herself.

Before he joined them, SP29 said, "Of course. How else did you think we're going to perform brain surgery?"

She looked away as the blade started to whirr. A horrible, squelching noise sounded, and she guessed it was cutting into his skull. Keeping her eyes on the deck, she muttered, "I don't know." Tears blurred her vision and dropped to land on her nearly bare feet.

"Hannah." SP29's voice was soft. "Look at me. Don't look at the pod."

She did so, meeting his hazel gaze. Understanding was reflected there. "Yeah?"

"We're doing this for you two," he said quietly. "This isn't our usual way. If he'd collapsed while we were cruising open space, we would have begun cloning procedures immediately and discarded . . ." Something in Hannah's expression stopped him from finishing that sentence. "We would have simply cloned him and started anew," he finished.

"Do you think you can save him? I don't want him to not be Rhys anymore."

"I don't know. But if we can't, we're going to clone him. It's what he would have wanted."

"Is it?" The bitter words escaped her before she could talk herself out of them.

SP29 hesitated. "RH103 would have wanted that. I don't know about Rhys. Look, Hannah, I have to help now.

Stay here, and don't look at us while we're working. There's going to be a lot of blood."

Her stomach clenched at the thought of Rhys bleeding out. All she could do to keep from crying was nod and turn away.

———

HANNAH WAS unsure how much time passed as the other cyborgs worked on Rhys. The silence in the sickbay was overwhelming. Part of her wanted to scream—to let out her frustration at feeling so useless and just to see if her reaction would be noticed. It was a foolish notion, but persistent. She wasn't sure she could handle losing another person she loved ever again.

She should have told him how she felt. She thought they had time, that they could have what passed for a normal relationship on New Eden. As soon as he woke up, she would tell him.

A wet splat from the direction of Rhys's pod had her nerves even further on edge. "Fuck!" she yelped. A couple of cyborgs looked up in her direction, their expressions smooth and impassive as those of dolls. She still had the impression that she'd irritated them.

A hand on her arm drew another yelled epithet from her. She turned around to face Jasmine, her face drawn. "Come on," she said.

Hannah pulled her arm away. "No."

"You can't do anything while they're operating." The wet squelch sounded again, making Hannah glad she couldn't see as they drilled into his skull. "Come with me. They'll tell us what's going on when they're done."

"Fuck you." The curse was weak-sounding and she

immediately regretted it. Her friend's face blurred through her tears. "I'm sorry. I didn't mean that."

"Yes, you did, and that's okay. We still need to get out of here and let them do their work."

This time, Hannah let Jasmine drag her out of the sickbay and through the bowels of the ship. She didn't let go of Hannah's hand, knowing she needed the support. They didn't stop until they were in the ship's bridge, its screens and controls dark. Weak light shone from panels in the ceiling. They sat down in a pair of seats next to each other in the center of the bridge. "Do you want to talk?" Jasmine asked.

Hannah hesitated. She did, but she was unsure how to voice her worries. Finally, she said, "I don't want to lose him too."

"Of course, you don't. They'll save him." Despite her encouraging words, there was a waver in Jasmine's voice.

"I don't want to hear about how they'll just make another Rhys if he dies."

"I wasn't going to say that."

Hannah sniffled. "I'm sorry, I know you wouldn't try to tell me a bunch of bullshit about how RH104 would be the same person." She dabbed at her eyes with her T-shirt's hem. "I can't deal with losing someone else. I've been bracing myself against it since the quake, afraid to be normal again in case we have another disaster."

"Hannah . . ."

She forged on, cutting off Jasmine. "No, I need to say this. I've been working like a fucking dog in the fields because it's easier than grieving." Not that they'd had dogs on New Eden since she was a little girl, but that was irrelevant. "I've pushed away you and Rodelle because it would be easier to grieve if either of you died in another quake or from something that's preventable everywhere else in the universe. I've had walls around me for years and couldn't take them down."

"Until Rhys showed up."

She hated having to admit that. "Until he showed up, yeah. God, I'm terrible for that."

"No, you aren't. Rhys and the others represented the first shred of hope we've had in years, if not our lives. That's why you felt it was okay to fall in love with him."

"And you don't represent hope? You're my best friend!"

"I told you before, I'm not upset about that. Grief does weird things to people. Maybe now that we have a chance at actually rebuilding our society, we can pick up where we left off. You know where I live."

That drew a small smile from Hannah. "Thank you."

"Come here." Before she could react, Jasmine reached across their seats to take her into an awkward hug. "He'll get through this," she said into her hair. "Darius said he has every faith that they can complete this surgery successfully."

"Which one is Darius again, and how does Darius know?"

"The dark-haired cyborg who used to be DL16, the one with the great shoulders. SP29 told him through their mind link thing, then Darius told me what happened when we were sorting through chicken embryos, and I ran here as soon as I could."

"Thank you." She reached for Jasmine's hand and squeezed it. "I missed you, you know. I'm glad you're here. Rhys would be, too, if he could wake up."

"In his way, I'm sure." Jasmine squeezed back affectionately. "Now, do you want to wait here or go back to your house? Or mine? I'm sure someone will tell us as soon as Rhys is out of surgery."

Whether that surgery would be successful or not

remained to be seen. Hannah had never waited on tenter-hooks like this before, and she wasn't sure how to do that now. "I think I'd like to stay."

Jasmine appeared unruffled by her words. "Then, that's what we'll do."

———

THE BABBLE of voices in his head, a cacophony of murmurs, shouts, and orders over Rhys's condition as they tried to revive him, was maddening. Rhys wished for nothing more than to stand up and stretch, work the tension out of his muscles.

No, he realized. What he wanted to do most was hold Hannah again.

He wished he could tell his fellow cyborgs what was wrong—that the sensors implanted in his cerebellum and hippocampus needed to be replaced. His internal proces-sors tallied up a list of everything that had gone wrong in his body, the reminders scrolling across his mind. He knew his eyes were open, but he couldn't see anything.

A memory fragment crossed his mind, so fleeting he nearly missed it. He concentrated, trying to tune out the noise around him to focus on it. His cybernetic functions forced his lungs to breathe, a strange sensation for someone used to it being automatic. He hadn't realized he'd been holding on to his breath until now. That had to be a good sign. He was still in charge of some of his bodily functions.

The memory bloomed in his mind in bright, ugly color. The original Rhys, preparing for . . . a battle? He saw himself strapping weaponry to his body and setting his cybernetic functions on high alert. Rhys saw the sterile room in which he was preparing, a few familiar faces around him as they did the same. "Not everyone will get through this alive," his original said in the memory. A murmur of agreement sounded through the crowd. "Death is better than what we're living now."

The original stomped through the room to a corridor, then into an open field. If he could shudder in his pod, he would have. He recognized the field, surrounded by lights on tall poles. This was where the original Rhys was executed.

To his original's surprise, he was greeted with a battalion of black-uniformed soldiers, weapons aimed squarely at him and his fellow cyborgs. It took a few seconds for Rhys to recognize the weapons were energy disruptors. Before he could call out a warning to his men, they were fired upon. His original fell to the ground as the pulse threw his systems offline. A familiar black shadow fell over him. This time, when Rhys looked up, he could see the face of a hard-edged man in his late fifties, quiet fury written across his features. He'd been cybernetically enhanced, too, but the tech in his skin looked older, as if he was a prototype. While Rhys couldn't place a name to him, he instinctively knew this man was his commanding officer in a battalion from hell. "What you're describing is a coup," the man said, voice low and tinged with rage.

"I was not brought on to this project for these reasons. What you're doing is inhumane. None of these people signed up for this," his original said. His voice was strong, but there was an undercurrent of fear in it. Rhys knew his original understood that death was imminent for him.

Rhys desperately wanted to wake up, to never experience his own death again, but at the same time, he needed to know why he was cloned in the first place. His lungs whooshed out another rush of air. Dimly, he heard SP29's panicked, "Sensors!"

"You signed up to do whatever you were told to. Today, that order was to mine the Darraugh Sector for darzanite."

"There are colonists there already with intergalactic rights to the mines." The original's voice was still steady.

"They're Pelossians." The commanding officer's voice held a note of disdain.

"The Pelossians have refused trade with us."

"No matter. They will do as they are told and turn over the mines, or they will die. So will you."

His original shook his head. "No."

"No?" The officer sighed. "I didn't think you were this soft, Hammond." To one of the other soldiers, he said, "Kill him."

His original looked up at the officer, whose hands, studded with ports, reached for him. Before he could blink, his body froze, every system failing. Everything turned dark, spots forming in his vision as he slid to the ground.

Rhys tensed. His automatic functions took over, forcing him to breathe again.

A rainbow of colors burst in front of his vision, like a star gone nova. His breathing slowed and heart rate returned to normal, as if he'd resumed his regular sleep patterns. Image fragments danced through his mind, pieces of memories he couldn't recall before now. He saw his original's life in its entirety for the first time, as if he had lived those experiences himself. Saw the intergalactic war that had spurred the creation of the cyborg program. His role in it, hideous as it was. His successful bargaining on behalf of his fellow enhanced soldiers for better pay and working conditions. And finally, his realization at what his troop was doing, the pain and suffering they inflicted on others. Shame flowed through him at those memories.

Finally, he saw the cyborg uprising he'd instigated. He saw his original getting shot again. Another memory of waking up in a fluid-filled tank resurfaced, and he knew he was watching his first successful clone.

A jolt of what felt like raw power sizzled up his spine. Rhys opened his eyes, blinking against bright light. Had he been cloned again? Was he being resurrected as RH104? He tried to speak, but the words didn't come.

"Shhh." The voice was familiar. "You've been through a lot. It might take a few minutes for your larynx to work again."

Work . . .again? Did that mean he hadn't been cloned, that he was still in his 103rd body? Rhys swallowed. At least that was functioning. "Hnnn."

"I said *shhh*." A dark shape filled his vision. For half a second, Rhys thought it was his executioner. He blinked and saw it was SP29. "We replaced malfunctioning sensors in your brain."

Rhys licked his lips. "Hippocampus," he croaked.

"And your cerebellum. What did I say about talking?"

A dry cough escaped him. "Fuck you."

SP29 smiled thinly. "There's that charming personality again. Don't try to move too much. Your head is still healing. We had to break it open."

"It would've been easier to clone me again." As much as Rhys hated to admit that, it was the fastest way to heal a cyborg with failing brain components.

"Hannah might have killed me if I'd done that."

The mention of Hannah made his heart lurch in a way that had nothing to do with his cybernetics. "Where is she?"

"Aboard the ship. She's in the cockpit with Jasmine."

"Can you get her?"

SP29 didn't need to be asked twice. He left the sickbay faster than Rhys had ever seen him move. Whether it was because of Rhys's recovery or an excuse to see Jasmine, he couldn't say. Despite the gravity of the situation, he couldn't help but smile. The motion made his head hurt. Cringing, he gingerly touched his temple. He felt smooth skin, where his hair had been shaved, and a thin line, where his skull had been sutured. His cybernetics tallied up a damage report and it skated across his vision. The chips in his brain had critically failed, accounting for his memory lapses and physical collapses.

He heard Hannah's weeping before he saw her. He wished he could get up to comfort her but didn't dare move just yet. Her tear-streaked face loomed over him, terror in her eyes. "Oh, my God!"

"I'm fine now," he said.

"You look like you've been ripped apart and sewn back together!"

"I was."

"Thank God for that." She buried her face into his shoulder, sobs wracking her body. "They didn't clone you again!"

"I would still be gestating in the tank if I'd been cloned." He lifted an arm to hold her, his head protesting at the movement.

She lifted her head and sniffled. "I thought you were going to die. I couldn't handle it. I don't think I can go through losing someone I love again."

Rhys's heart skipped a beat. He looked around the room at the neutral expressions of his fellow cyborgs. "Leave us," he commanded. SP29 bit back a smile and looked away before leaving. The others remained rooted to the floor. "Go," Rhys repeated. "Come back in five minutes."

They finally shuffled out, leaving Rhys and Hannah alone.

"I wish I'd told you that before," she whispered.

"It's all right. I love you too." He'd never said those words to anyone, nor was he certain his original had, either.

"I'll tell you every day from now on," she promised. "Just please don't fall apart on me like that again."

"My sensors have been replaced with new units. It won't happen again." He hauled himself to a sitting position, wincing a little as he did so. "Hannah, come here."

She threw herself into his arms. "I was so scared!"

"So was I. While I was out, I remembered everything. I know why we exist. I'll have to tell the others about it. I know they've been wondering."

"Is it bad?" she asked tentatively.

He nodded. "Our originals weren't good people. They eventually realized where they had gone wrong, but not before our unit brought destruction across the galaxy." He stroked her hair, reveling in her familiar scent. One he'd thought he'd never smell again while he was being operated on. "I love you so much, Hannah Forsyth."

"I love you too."

He sighed, hating to speak his next words. "You may not, when you find out what we did."

———

RHYS SWAYED a little on his feet at first. Hannah reached out to steady him when he hauled himself out of his sickbay pod. He grasped her hand, and to her surprise, brought her to him for a kiss in front of the other cyborgs. Her free hand flew up to touch his face, to make sure he was really all right. His short dark hair had been shaved off, and thin scars bisected his scalp. He turned to everyone assembled, opened his mouth to speak, then paused, as if unsure what to say. Finally, he said, "Did any of you pick up on the dreams I was having while I was in surgery?"

"I could tell you were experiencing something similar to REM sleep, but our equipment registered the phenomenon as unknown. We couldn't read what you were experiencing," SP29 replied. There was a murmur of agreement from the others.

"I recalled my original's memories while I was out," Rhys announced.

Hannah thought she could hear everyone in the room stop breathing for a second. His warning that she might not love him after he told her what his original had done rang through her mind like a alarm.

"As we suspected, our originals were recruited for military operations," he continued. He leaned against the pod's side and rolled his shoulders, as if to physically shake off bad memories. "Rhys Hammond was the leader of our troop. He was a black ops specialist, recruited for top secret jobs around the old world. His specialties were off-world espionage and black market trade. He was especially adept in rooting out illegal arms dealers.

"A counterintelligence agency recruited him after they developed a super soldier program. He was paid to recruit other candidates to the program, too, most of whom are your originals. Hammond and the others thought they were to be proverbial guinea pigs and were compensated accordingly, until they were ordered to invade the Darraugh Sector for their darzanite."

Hannah had never heard of either of those things, but the others nodded. "Darraugh has been uninhabited for years," SP29 said.

"In part, due to the program's invasion and mining efforts. The entire sector is unlivable. Pelossian settlers were in the process of terraforming an H-class planet when the original cyborg troop was ordered to put a stop to it and take over the mining operations on behalf of an Earther corporation that wanted first access to it. Hammond refused to be involved with the mass murder of the Pelossians and tipped them off, causing an evacuation. Then he led an uprising of the other originals against the program's director. He was executed for it."

The room was again silent. "What about the rest of the originals?"

Rhys gave a half shrug. Pain bracketed lines around his eyes and mouth. Whether it was because of his surgery or the memories flowing back, Hannah had no idea. "I don't know. It's possible they were executed as well, and the first clones were ordered to the Darraugh Sector. The darzanite was mined until there was nothing left. Some of our previous iterations may have worked in the mines. I don't know for sure."

"Wouldn't any of us remember that?" one of them asked. It took Hannah a few seconds to remember his name. Brandon something? She recalled Rhys telling her he'd taken a different one from his original's.

"Not necessarily. I'm the only one who has consistently had memories from my past selves turn up. I wish our records aboard the ship were still intact."

"If they were there in the first place. Our previous clones bought it and retrofitted it about thirty years ago, after we settled on our homeworld," Brandon piped up. To Rhys, he said, "Do you have any idea how long ago our originals existed? We've all agreed it has to be at least thirty or forty years ago."

Rhys hesitated. Hannah's heart pounded against her ribs. She knew that look. He had an answer and wasn't sure if everyone else would like it. "My original was murdered nine months after he entered the cyborg program, two hundred and four years ago," he finally replied.

A dozen pairs of wide eyes stared at him. "That long?" SP29 finally said.

Rhys nodded. "I don't remember much of the other clones, other than my first and last one. My first clone drowned." Where he'd drowned, and the reason why he was in the water in the first place, still eluded him. Drowning did explain his terror of being in the water at the power station. They all remembered his last clone's death, when his cybernetic heart gave out. It was the first and last time they'd tried using a non-organic heart in a cyborg.

"We have something to work with as far as our origins," Brandon pointed out.

Rhys's reply was anguished. "We do, but this proves that we were built for terrible purposes. All of our originals were complicit with murder and who knows what else."

"We suspected as much already. We also know now that our originals refused to participate," SP29 said firmly. "They did something right."

"What about their first generations of clones? They did as they were told."

"Up to a point. It stands to reason that the first generation of clones rebelled as well. Maybe the second generation. Maybe they rebelled earlier than our originals did," SP29 countered. "They would have inherited the same personality traits our originals had, which included shreds of morality. If anything, their innate moral senses increased, because they hadn't spent years of their lives chasing gunrunners for hire."

Rhys looked surprised at SP29's vehement answer. Hannah squeezed his hand and gave him a look that she hoped was reassuring. He was wrong about her not loving him after hearing that story. She'd suspected from the beginning that their originals hadn't been entirely decent people.

"You've been minding your own business for years," Hannah said, speaking for the first time. "You went out of your way to help us here."

"In exchange for a home," Rhys bit out.

"And you were ready to leave us if we said no. You were still going to help us if we said no. Those aren't the markers of awful people." She surveyed those assembled. "And you're all people to us, not just clones. You're people first, and I'm glad you're part of our community." To Rhys, she asked, "Can you walk?"

He nodded, confusion written across his face.

"Do you need to stay here for recovery, or can you sleep it off at home?"

"We replaced your sensors entirely. Your nanobots should be back online," SP29 told Rhys.

"Everything has come back online," Rhys reported.

"I think we should regularly replace those sensors, as long as we're in our current bodies. Yours were the oldest ones implanted, and I'm sure everyone else will see theirs break down over the coming months and years," SP29 said. He rolled his shoulders. "At least, as long as we want to stay in these bodies. Someone might want to be cloned again down the road, I don't know."

"What about cloned organs or blood?" Jasmine's voice made Hannah jump. So focused on Rhys, she hadn't even noticed her friend nearby.

SP29's voice and expression softened when he looked at her. "Of course. That's an essential part of New Eden's medical care now."

Hannah wondered if his look had gone unnoticed by

the others. She brushed it aside, focusing on the matter at hand and the man next to her.

"I want to tell everyone else on New Eden about our origins," Rhys said. "They have a right to know."

Hannah nodded. God only knew how they would react to that piece of news.

He squeezed her hand, a motion that warmed her heart. It was a reminder that he was truly all right now. "They have the right to make an informed decision about our staying here, now that we have a better idea of why we exist."

"They might riot if we call yet another meeting at the amphitheater," Jasmine muttered. Hannah bit back a smile.

Hannah faced Rhys. His expression was grim, despite his positive prognosis. "Let's get on that," she said. "We'll have another meeting tonight, let's say, six o'clock. Until then, you need to be back in bed."

"The landing pad and launch tower are still in need of repairs," he protested.

"Oh, my God, Rhys, you just had brain surgery! You're going home!" She caught a few smiles hidden behind hands and Jasmine's wide grin after she said the words.

"Listen to her, Rhys," Brandon said.

Rhys sighed, then pulled her to him in a hug. "I'll go home," he murmured into her hair. "As long as it's still our home."

"Of course it is." She sank into his heat, knowing she would never take his arms around her for granted again. "It wouldn't be home without you."

EPILOGUE

The launch tower and landing pad were as complete as they could get for now. New comp systems were necessary to complete the rebuild, and all the components would have to be sourced from somewhere else. Rhys had put together lists of the needed supplies and the closest places to get them, leaving SP29 in charge of procurement. He was glad to receive that assignment. He needed to get the hell away from New Eden for a while.

He hadn't worried about the backlash Rhys had warned them about when the New Edeners learned about their origins. SP29 had spent more time working alongside them than Rhys, who cozied up to Hannah as soon as they met. Jealousy flared through him when he thought about the connection those two shared, their fierce love for each other as they built a life together, warring with complex feelings he had for two other people. Once upon a time, it had just been DL16, now called Darius. Now, it was Darius *and* Jasmine.

If he had to stay on New Eden any longer, he would

snap. He needed some time away, to work them out of his system and get his shit together. SP29 wasn't so sure he'd ever had it together in his current iteration. Maybe his previous clones had, or his original, he had no idea. Nor did he care any longer.

He decided to leave New Eden for the nearest waystation in the early morning, before everyone else rose for the day. He didn't want his leaving to turn into a spectacle, with lots of hugs and well-wishes for a trip that would see him back on New Eden soil in a week. A few cyborgs had volunteered to accompany him, those who were smart enough not to get caught up in romantic entanglements like he had.

His crew was lined up outside the ship, waiting for him, as dawn crested in the sky. The twin suns rose in the horizon, the larger one slightly faster. SP29 wasn't sure if he would have noticed that detail without his enhanced vision. Vision which had to be playing tricks on him, because Darius was waiting there with the rest of them. His heart squeezed in a way that had nothing to do with faulty cybernetics. This wasn't good.

"Good morning," he said to everyone assembled. He counted six, including Darius. "I was only expecting five crew," he said to him. SP29 scanned his face, looking for any traces of deception or trickery and found none.

Darius shrugged. "It's been a long time since we've been to a waystation, and I have a few things I want to pick up. Besides, you can use the help. I saw that list Rhys gave you. There's a *lot* of stuff."

He was right, as loathe as SP29 was to admit it. He could use the help. "Fine," he ground out. "Come with us, then."

Darius's expression remained neutral at the sharp reply, but he didn't comment on it. SP29 hoped he wouldn't have to have difficult talks with about their relationship—or lack thereof— during this trip, at least. He couldn't handle any more secret heartbreak.

"Hey!"

SP29's body went cold at the sound of the female voice calling behind him. His data readout in the lower corner of his vision reported that the effect was psychological. No shit. He turned around to see Jasmine running toward the ship, an old straw tote bag slipping off her shoulder. "No," he said quietly, knowing she couldn't hear him.

"She really wants to come along," Darius said.

SP29 knew that, because she had asked about it the night before over supper. He'd refused then and would do it again now.

"You nearly left without me," Jasmine said indignantly when she reached them. She hauled up the strap to the bag, a shirt sleeve hanging out the side.

"We did, because this is strictly a cyborg trip." SP29 regretted the words almost as soon as he said them. He wanted to put distance between them to protect his own heart, not hurt her.

"But there's nothing wrong with me going, other than you don't want me to go?" The hurt in her voice pulled at him. "Plus, you promised I could go with you on this supply trip."

"It wouldn't be fun," SP29 replied.

"How the hell would it not be fun? I've never left New Eden! Just being on your ship in outer space sounds fun!" Her outraged look would have been comical if she wasn't so angry. "I don't even have to leave the ship if it isn't safe. I can stay aboard and just experience not being stuck planetside for a few days."

"Let her come along," Darius wheedled.

SP29 arched an eyebrow at his direction. "Is this your doing?"

"No, but I may have been the one to tell her when the ship was leaving."

"I set an alarm. I'm a heavy sleeper," Jasmine piped up.

SP29 asked via their shared broadcast link if the others minded her tagging along. A chorus of nos resounded in his head. He sighed. "We don't have much in the way of comforts aboard the ship. I think there may be a cot somewhere."

"I can sleep anywhere."

"Even upright in a recharging pod?"

Jasmine's smile faltered. "No. A cot will work, though. Or a chair. I just really want to see what's out there." Her hopeful look returned. SP29's gaze flickered between her and Darius, both of them giving him expectant looks.

Damn it, why did both of them have to be so attractive? "Hot" was how Jasmine described attractive people. SP29 liked the term. "Does anyone else know you'll be with us, or is this a spur-of-the-moment thing?" SP29 asked.

Jasmine looked like she was ready to jump up and down in excitement. She already knew she'd worn him down. "I told Rodelle and left a note for Hannah on her door."

"Rodelle's awake?" SP29 rarely saw the widow of New Eden's late mayor.

"Rodelle sleeps at weird hours." Jasmine gave him an odd look, clearly questioning why he was asking. "Can I go with you?"

He had no real reason to say no, other than his heart felt like it would break every time he looked at her or Darius. Being aboard the ship with both of them for days would be torture. But he could hardly tell them that. His answer was terse. "Yes."

Her face lit up like a star going nova. "Yes! Thank you!"

As SP29 activated the ship's exterior ramp, he couldn't help but wonder if he was making a bigger mistake than he originally anticipated. He waited until the others boarded before bringing up the rear, noting with envy the easy way Darius and Jasmine laughed and joked with each other. He waited until the others left the airlock before he ordered the ramp retracted and the door shut, then followed them to the bridge.

This was going to be the longest trip he'd ever taken.

ABOUT THE AUTHOR

Jessica Marting is a sci-fi and paranormal romance author, art enthusiast (not quite an artist, despite all that time in art school), an avid reader, and makeup collector. She lives in Toronto.

Sign up for her newsletter at jessicamarting.com/newsletter for pre-order alerts, sales, freebies, and more.

Magic & Mechanicals

Wolf's Lady

Sea Change

Bound in Blood

Dragon's Keep

Spellbound

The Searchers

Blood Ties

Blood Moon

Blood Virtue

Zone Cyborgs

Haven

Paradise

Oasis

Safe Harbor

Sanctuary

Refuge

The Commons

Supernova

Celestial Chaos

Standalone Novels & Novellas

Spindle's End

Trade Secrets

Neon Vice

Dead Ringer

Rapture

Escape From Europa 10

Castaways

Demon's Favor

Her Purrfect Match